HETEROSIS

A novel about a blending of two cultures.

R.B. RAIKOW

Gotham Books

30 N Gould St.
Ste. 20820, Sheridan, WY 82801
https://gothambooksinc.com/

Phone: 1 (307) 464-7800

© 2023 *R.B. Raikow*. All rights reserved.

No part of this book may be reproduced, stored in a retrieval system, or transmitted by any means without the written permission of the author.

Published by Gotham Books (September 26, 2023)

ISBN: 979-8-88775-403-1 (P)
ISBN: 979-8-88775-404-8 (E)

Because of the dynamic nature of the Internet, any web addresses or links contained in this book may have changed since publication and may no longer be valid.

The views expressed in this work are solely those of the author and do not necessarily reflect the views of the publisher, and the publisher hereby disclaims any responsibility for them.

TABLE OF CONTENTS

1 Calling 1
2 Mission 5
3 A New World 8
4 Searching.. 10
5 Negotiations 11
6 Island Forum... 13
7 Frustration 16
8 Invitation... 19
9 Meeting 22
10 An Old friend.. 25
11 Resentment 28
12 Determination... 30
13 Two Souls... 33
14 Confirmation.. 39
14 An Ally 42
15 Documentation 46
16 Obstacles 49
17 Persuasion 53
18 A New Ally 57
19 Roots.. 60
20 Common Cause 64
21 Bored Board 70
22 Nadir.. 75
23 Ad Hoc Forum 78
24 Serra Club.. 80
25 An Offer 83
26 Production 88
27 Confrontation 90
28 Courtroom 94
29 A Valuable Player 99
30 Resolution 102
31 In Their Element.. 104
32 Celebration 110

1
Calling

Raisha stormed out of the campus science building, in which she had spent more years than she cared to admit. She blinked at the bright sunshine, a contrast to the dark hall where she just had a discussion with her advisor and some fellow students. "I'll never hire a woman for an important post unless she's ugly or has her tubes tied," the professor had said. He was young and apparently progressive. *If he meant it as a joke it was a stupid one,* she thought. *Does he think that women are just baby machines?* Then she remembered her mother, who had devoted all her life to raising her children and now seemed lost after her children had moved away.

She pushed open the massive, brass doors of the main library building. She always felt at peace there - so may thoughts being absorbed by many minds, she mused. *I wonder if it's recorded yet?* At the first free computer monitor, she entered: "Variations in Chironomid Pheromones; PhD Thesis, Endicott, Raisha". She clenched her fist triumphantly when her file appeared. Then, feeling a twinge of nostalgia about not going to her usual study cubicle, she walked outside carrying the sleek attache case, which her parents had given her as a graduation present. With her slim, twenty-five-year-old frame and long light-brown hair, tied in a pony tail, she easily passed as a student or a young instructor. The elegant attache case, incongruent with her jeans and tee shirt, held only her lunch now.

Reaching her favorite spot on the large campus, under a grove of giant, evergreen trees, she laid down on the soft needles carpeting the floor, and looked up at the branches above. They wafted a fresh smell in the warm sun and made a hypnotic hum with the gentle breeze. The sound of a nearby stream grew louder.

She got up to investigate. To her surprise she found the stream different from the one she knew. Bending down to the water she spotted colorful little frogs and fishes. This is a tropical stream! How can it be? Then she turned toward a clanging sound behind her, and saw a bulldozer pushing dirt toward her. On the machine were seated her former professors sipping tea from delicate cups. Are you crazy? That dirt will destroy the life in this stream, she tried to yell...

The absurdity of the image, as well as the chiming of the campus clock, woke her up. *I must be getting old. I've never dozed off like this before in the middle of the day. What a combination: destruction of nature, and silly professors. What could be the connection in my mind? I guess some professors are oblivious to the ecological problems of the world. Well so am I ...as long as I stay here.*

She stood, brushed debris off her jeans, and decided to check out a jobs bulletin board at the Student Union. As she walked to that building, she admired the large trees bordering her path, and thought: *I'm going to miss this campus.*

Posters advertising postgraduate study studded the board. She almost gave up, when a small typewritten note caught her eye: "Seeking a recent graduate to study use of natural products to control insect pests on Haraday Island. Salary to be determined, based on experience." Excited, she scribbled the information on an envelope.

"Hi honey," a familiar hand rubbed her shoulder. "You don't need to search for a job," Jack said cheerfully. "You will always have a place with me!" His presumption annoyed her. He did not notice her frown, and continued: "I have been offered an apprenticeship with a wonderful firm in San Francisco. Wouldn't you like to live where '"little cable cars reach up to the stars'?" He was tan and handsome, a dream combination of looks and smarts, but just then she almost felt like slapping him. Still there was too much history between them for her to dismiss him. (Jack and Raisha had been an item for the past three years, and their peers assumed they were a permanent pair. They did not share professional interests, since he was in law school, but they had the same idealistic concern about the welfare of the world. He was a gentle lover and had apparently honest feelings toward her.)

She felt the time had come to assert her independence. She took his hand and led him to a table. "I'm going to apply for this job," she said as she resolutely pushed a slip of paper toward him. His face knitted into a pout. She considered trying to explain her feelings, but then just said simply: "I feel this place calling me."

He studied her for a while and then said lightheartedly. "Well, the South Pacific does have wonderful weather. Go and get it out of your system, honey."

Raisha's familiarity with insect pheromones was the selling point that got her the job. Her idea was that pheromones could be used as lures for trapping insect pests without having to spread any chemicals on the crops. It was a long shot but it was based on a hope, prominent in the mind of Dr. Verner, the research director at the experimental station on the island, that natural products should be used whenever possible.

Her salary was only enough to pay for food and necessities, and she was assigned a free room in a dormitory. Given her youth and health it did not occur to her to ask about health insurance or retirement benefits. Her many years at school taught her to have modest expectations in the material realm, and she hoped to reap rewards of satisfaction in doing something important for the environment.

2
Mission

To the north of Haraday, on another, much smaller island, a seductive rhythm of drums reverberated past thatched-roof huts, signaling the beginning of day.

Iakano rolled over on his hemp hammock, rubbed his eyes and got up without hesitation. He cleaned his teeth by chewing a special root, which he had collected for that purpose. *Amazingly this really works*, he thought. Then he worked his way through lush vegetation to a central hut, acknowledging the warm greetings of his neighbors.

A year ago Iakano had ventured to the mainland. Now he was grateful that he had been accepted back by his people. The insistent drums made his heart beat faster. *I must not miss the opening chant.*

"Aloha", called a large woman with a garland made of fragrant flowers around her neck, as she took a position alongside a rock altar before one large hut. "Aloha", answered the people gathered before her.. Three men and three women came out of the main hut carrying a bamboo palanquin on which sat a representation of a large bird. It was covered with orange feathers, with long flowing feathers forming its tail. All eyes fixed on the object as it was placed on a stone altar. The rays of the morning sun made the statue seem to glow. They moved respectfully aside, to allow the large woman stand beside it.

"Anara, god of life, keep us safe and content throughout this day," she chanted. Then all repeated the short prayer. Iakano marveled at its simplicity, a contrast to the long-winded sermons he remembered.

The statue was returned to the relatively large temple hut, and the day's work began. Various groups set out to gather food, while others wove mats or prepared the day's meal. Iakano resumed carving a canoe from a large tree trunk. He was proud of his ability to do this ancient task, using only sharpened fragments of pottery.

An old neighbor came over to visit him. (It had taken almost a year after his return for his neighbors to become so friendly.) The man bent down and ran his hand over the curve of the unfinished canoe. He was the local medical authority, expert in the use of herbs. Iakano was aware that a man in the village had recently become ill so he inquired: "How is your patient?"

The old man bowed his head sadly. "Please invoke Anara for him." (This fixation on Anara, god of life and healing, had been hard for Iakano to take seriously, until one day he got relief from his migraines, after the medicine man laid hands on him while chanting to the bird-god.) "We need the living spirits with us," the medicine man continued, "Pray that the new foray-mission will succeed."

Iakano's stomach knotted. He knew well what the foray mission meant, and it brought back some of the anxiety that he had lately started to shed. Not wishing to offend, he nodded and said: "I'll see you later at the blessing." He tried to block out thoughts of the large island and the mainland that came flooding into his mind. He furiously worked the tools on the hard wood of the emerging canoe, but it was no use. So he went into his hut, laid down and closed his eyes.

He saw himself walking along a white beach, and spotting a woman with light hair bent over collecting something in shallow pools. As he approached, she straightened and beckoned him to follow. They entered a wooden structure, where young men and women were lying around on large pillows. The air was thick with acrid smoke. He felt dizzy. He tried to leave but the woman pulled him down and offered him a joint.... Next he was carving out a canoe again, but this time he had metal tools. A man came over and gave him some money. Finally he was launching his finished canoe. The waves tossed him. He lurched forward and woke up.

When the work day was over, all the people on the small island gathered in a clearing. Iakano stood in the back. Three strong men, volunteers for the planned foray in search of the living Anara, knelt before the presider, who laid her hands on each of the volunteer's heads, and said: "May all the gods bless you and bring you back to us safely".

There was a communal meal that evening, in which the three men were fed especially delicious fish and fruit. In the morning all gathered on the beach as the three set out in a slender canoe packed with dried fish, fruits, nuts and bamboo spears for fishing. They deftly maneuvered the canoe between white-capped waves, and once in the sea beyond the breakers they waved. Everyone waved back, with somewhat muted smiles. These sendoffs, ventured periodically, were yet to succeed. Still all the people agreed that they were important.

3
A New World

In a valley on Faraday Island, a plowed field with rows of small plants, contrasted with the palm forest around it. Next to the field was a dingy greenhouse, where two men in jeans sat on an overturned tub.

Dr. Verner, a trim man, dressed in khakis and a conservative Aloha shirt, walked briskly with an air of authority. Raisha followed him. She felt hot and sweaty despite the cool cotton dress she wore. The director proceeded to introduce everyone: "This is our grounds crew, and this is Dr. Endicott, the newest member of our research team. She will be setting up some experiments in the field. Please give her total cooperation."

The two men, sitting sprawled on the makeshift bench, exchanged glances. Raisha, now even more uncomfortable as she noticed their concentration on her chest, tried to shield her eyes from the sun with one hand as she offered her other to the two. They just nodded.

Later surveying some dried up plants on the counters of the greenhouse, Raisha had misgivings about taking the job to work there. But then she resolved to make the best of it. *Faraday is a wonderful island, and I have much to explore.*

At the Experimental Center's small library she searched for helpful background information. She scanned entries under the heading, "Recent research at the Waioo Agricultural Station: "Tomato Mutation for Easier Shipping"; "Survey of Insect Pests in Sugar Cane Fields"; "Survey of Insect Pests in Pineapple Fields"; "Marketing Strategies for Island Produce"; "Birds as Controls of Common Pests." She clicked on the last entry, only to find another simple survey, but one line of it caught her eye. It read, "Unfortunately, none of the native birds, touted by some as the best insect predators, have been seen here since 1958."

There were no entries dealing with insect pheromones, her area of expertise, so she decided to search entries from a nearby college. (This was a branch of a university from the mainland with an associated hospital.) Most of the entries there were papers comparing the incidence of diseases in the native and immigrant human populations. Then she found a study using mass spectroscopy to trace insecticides in field worker's blood. So she decided to contact those authors, reasoning that they might help her to separate and purify chemicals she wanted to test for their pheromone effectiveness.

4
Searching

With muscles glistening from sweat and ocean spray, three young men strained to steer their canoe between the waves as it approached Haraday's shore. Moving along at a safe distance from the shore, they anxiously eyed the coast, where newcomer buildings almost blotted out everything else.

At last they reached a part of the coast where a pristine-looking beach was surrounded by tall mountains. It seemed inaccessible by land, so they pulled into shore. Reassured by its emptiness, they hid their canoe in some vegetation, where they found a small spring. After they quenched their thirst they agreed to meet by their canoe in the evening and dispersed in different directions.

Their hardened bare feet made walking in the underbrush easy. They made soft birdcalls, which echoed like the usual forest sounds. Often they would bend down to pick a berry or small a cluster of flowers, to comfort themselves with these reminders of home. Now and then they spotted a bird, but these sightings never included the object of their search.

After a week of searching the surrounding hillsides, they sadly returned home.

5
Negotiations

Raisha woke early. She surveyed the courtyard below her dormitory room. A gray bird with a bright red head alighted below her window. She quickly grabbed her guide to local fauna: "Crested Cardinal native of Brazil, now widely spread throughout the Pacific by man." *He is lovely,* she thought, *but did he displace some of the native species?*

She put on her jeans and a new tee shirt, with a tropical plant printed on the front. She wanted to look and feel her best, anticipating the meeting she had made for that morning. After brushing her teeth and hair in a communal bathroom, she went to the cafeteria holding her prepaid meal ticket. She tried to get mentally ready, knowing that it was important to give a good first impression. Her experience taught her that her original vision of scientists as people driven only by ideals, and always reaching for greater truth, was naive. She knew that it was best to go to the head of any research group to avoid being accused of spying or muscling in on new discoveries. Consequently, she had asked Dr. Verner, her supervisor, to arrange a meeting with the chairman of the Chemistry Department at the college.

The morning was cool as she walked to the college. Along the way she stooped to examine vegetation that still seemed exotic to her. *I guess I am a classical biologist at heart,* she thought, chuckling to herself over one of her advisor's comments, after she had admitted that chemistry courses were not her favorites: "If you want to be a butterfly collector, he said with a patronizing smile, "go right ahead and ignore my advice." As it turned out her thesis was an amalgam of ecology and chemistry. The main hall of the building had a smell she remembered from chemistry lab. She consulted a directory, and found the office of the chairman.

"I am Raisha Endicott and I have an appointment with Dr. Emery," she said to the secretary at the front. The door of the chairman's office was open, and he apparently heard her, for he stepped out with an outstretched hand. "Nice to meet you, Dr. Verner told me how excited he is over the prospect of your helping him with his project." (*Ouch,* thought Raisha. *I thought is was my project.*) Still, she was pleased that the chairman was enthusiastic and attentive. "Let me introduce you to the guy who can show you around." He motioned her ahead of him and led her across the hall.

Behind lab benches, crowded with equipment and glassware, sat a slight young man in front of a computer screen. As soon as the chairman walked in the door he jumped up and smiled. On the other side of the room two Asian men stopped their conversations. Dr Emery said, "Chuck, this is Dr. Endicott, Dr. Verner's new assistant. She'll be working here with us for a while and should have access to anything in the lab. Please give her any assistance required." Then the chairman left, and the smile faded from Chuck's face.

"What exactly is your position here, Chuck?" Asked Raisha, trying to start a conversation. He eyed her with a frown. "I just like to know whom I am dealing with," she continued, and immediately thought she should have phrased it better.

"I am a technician," Chuck said in an emotionless tone, "but I have been here long enough to amount to more than that. "After that brief exchange Chuck made a practice of avoiding Raisha, except to admonish her to better clean her work area. He was smart and able, but obviously preoccupied with moving up the ladder, apparently believing that Dr. Emery was his only means toward that end. Raisha witnessed that Chuck never refused or questioned any of his bosses requests, which well suited the overworked physician/chairman, who like everyone in academia, hoped to make it in research, despite his many administrative and clinical duties.

6
Island Forum

Children gathered Frangipani corollas, which had fallen off trees growing along the edge of their thatched hut village. They placed the fragrant blossoms around the chair designated for the leader of the month. Others brought fruits and nuts, folded into packages made of leaves, to share with their neighbors. All were anticipating a big meeting. The leader had spent the past four weeks hearing suggestions and complaints.

"This meeting is called to talk about our forays in search of the winged spirits of the sky," he said and raised his hand in a gesture that everyone recognized to be asking for comments.

"I don't like them," cried a young woman. Her loud voice surprised even her. She stood and looked around shyly.

"Come Alani", said the leader and offered her a spot at the head of the crowd.

"I think the trips to the other island are bad! We have lost many young men." Alani lowered her face and her doe eyes filled with tears.

Iakano stood, put his arm around her and led her back to her place. Then he turned to the others: "The men who don't come back from the searches are not dead. Instead they choose to stay among the newcomers." The crowd became agitated. Some of the youngest gasped incredulously, but the older ones sighed regretfully. Iakano felt he needed to explain. "I know this because I was one of those who had stayed." The hum of the crown rose louder, and he added defensively: "I am grateful that I was allowed to come back."

After all calmed down, an old woman got up. "The young ones don't understand how much the sacred, flying spirits mean to us." She raised her arms toward the sky. "Their presence is protection and even life itself. We all know of the fever many have suffered since the sacred spirits have not been seen." All nodded.

Another man added. "As the bird-gods protect us we must protect them! Some of them must still be on the other island, for it is bigger than ours. We know the newcomers are always increasing and so they threaten our bird-god."

"Does anyone else object to our continuing the foray-searches?" Asked the leader. All were silent. "Let us now hear from those who were on the last search." The three reported on details where to land, and on where they found edible plants and fresh water. They concluded: "This area seems to be free of all newcomers."

"We should not fear the newcomers. I know that there is good in some of them.," said Iakano.

"No one wants anything to do with them!" Shouted a man seated next to him.

Not deterred, Iakano continued" "I just thought that we should think about the possibility of having to deal with them. Then suddenly emboldened, he added: "I would like to go along with the next foray group."

"Do you really know the newcomer language?" asked the leader, and Iakano nodded. All sat in silence awaiting the leader's decision.

Finally the leader stood. "Dear Iakano we believe in your ability and sincerity to help. So you may accompany the next expedition, but remember there is not be to any contact with the newcomers, if it can be avoided. May Anara bless you!"

7
Frustration

Stepping out of her dorm, Raisha tried to concentrate on the tropical vegetation around her, as she walked to the chemistry lab. Then a very large cockroach on a piece of bark beside her path, made her think of Chuck, who was the one permanent feature in the lab, for the visiting students came and left frequently. *Wasn't Chuck supposed to show me the ropes?* She was sympathetic to his time constraints, but she couldn't help seeing the difference between the way he treated her, and other postdocs: He seemed happy to dole out help to them, while his dealings with her were perfunctory and dished out with thinly veiled contempt.

She had looked forward to their occasional lab meetings, hoping to participate in interesting discussions, but there was never a subject all could immediately own, because each, temporary member of the lab had a different agenda, and no time was ever spared for explanations to the uninitiated. The chairman, who presided occasionally, seemed to support Raisha's questions at first, but his administrative and clinical duties dominated his time. The lab's foreign students were reluctant to chime in on anything least bit controversial. They usually stayed only one year and felt long discussions might hinder their progress.

At first Raisha thought that there was just a personality conflict between her and Chuck. But then one day a young undergraduate volunteer sought her out in tears: "Why does chuck treat me as if I were an idiot?"

"Welcome to the club," said a visiting female scholar who was sharing the lunch table with them. "Chuck treats all females that way."

To her regret, Raisha never discussed the issue of Chuck's sexism with the chairman. Mainly because she was not secure enough about her status in the lab. (Things would have been different had she been really succeeding with her research.) She felt that, the chairman would not welcome her complaints, especially not complaints about Chuck, who constantly generated and delivered data on subjects in which the chairman was particularly interested.

As she approached the lab on a day of a scheduled, lab meeting, she made up her mind to encourage a positive spirit. She had prepared a list of problems she wanted to seek advice about.

"The meeting is cancelled!" Chuck informed her, as soon she walked in the door.

"Why?" She asked.

"There was no new business," he said curtly. Her disappointment turned into disgust. She recalled wistfully how in graduate school her fellow students were eager to discuss their research at each weekly meeting.

Unhappy, she returned to the experimental field. At least the grounds crew are usually pleasant. "Hi," she called and waved to one of them who was weeding among rows of pineapple plants.

"One of your little toys has fallen over in the north corner," he said pointing in that direction.

"Gee thanks, You are a dear. You know they are very important to me. So if you ever see one turned over again please call me right away...no matter what time it is."

"Gee I wish you cared that much about me," he said with a wink.

"You see," she tried to explain, "The length of time each one is operational is a very important part of the data I am collecting. I am trying..." She stopped because he held up his hand. She could tell from the bored expression growing on his face that trying to talk science with him was a waste of time.

"Gotta run!" He said.

She sighed watching him hurry away. Then, for each trap, she replenished the pheromone-like compounds that she had purchased from chemical supply firms. This was an attempt to get some results, while bypassing analysis of actual secretions of the local insects. Isolation of natural pheromones was proving difficult, not just because of the politics in the chemistry lab, but also because the amount of material that could be extracted from the native insects was miniscule.

8
Invitation

Lately her solitary walks were her only pleasures. So one sunny Saturday morning she decided to go for a really long hike. She packed food and water, enough for a day or two, into a backpack, tied a jacket around her waste and set out into the green hills overlooking the town. At first the going was easy because of paths worn by previous hikers, but then the underbrush grew thicker. Still Raisha continued to pick her way carefully among the roots and underbrush.

Deep in the forest she sat down on a patch of moss and leaned against a tree. *It was worth coming to this island just for this,* she thought. She drank from her canteen. The afternoon sun was making golden pools in the vegetation around her. Scanning the branches above she spotted to her delight, a lively orange bird.

It flew away. Then she caught sight of it it again, and its fluttering seemed to be inviting her to follow. She focused on the ground beneath her feet, and smiled at an iridescent beetle, cautiously stepping among delicate moss. It almost looked as if it was demonstrating how she should watch her step.

She felt happy and did not want to leave the forest. Had she been with her parents, or her mainland boyfriend, Jack, she would have been preached to about not venturing further and risking being lost in the dark. *So what's the worst that can happen?* Her biologist's training reassured her that there were no poisonous creatures or large predators around. She checked the provisions in her backpack. Resolved, she got up and and aimed in the direction in which the bird had flown. She stopped, now and then, to admire bright yellow shelf fungi and the variety of vines and mosses decorating everything.

A faint salty mist alerted her that the coast was near. The tree canopy thinned and finally disappeared. She found herself on the edge of a canyon overlooking a bay with a small beach. The view was idyllic: blue-green breakers, overhung by an azure sky, punctuated by fluffy clouds, beginning to take on the colors of sunset. She determined that it would be possible to descend toward the beach. Bird calls echoing in the canyon seemed to be inviting her to continue.

Suddenly she spotted another amazing orange bird. It was much larger than the one she had been pursuing. It swooped down and disappeared into the hillside below. Determined to see where it went she rushed down in the same direction. Her footing slipped occasionally on loose volcanic soil and she had to pause to rest. The ground was soft and warm as it conformed to her body.

She reached a ledge beside a cave whose entrance was festooned with delicate ferns. The sun was really setting now and she determined that this place would have to be her shelter for the night. Trying to make herself comfortable by cushioning a hollow with leaves in the back of the cave was largely futile, but finally she managed to drift off to sleep.

Four men struggled to maneuver their canoe toward the coast that was the destination specified by the previous search party. Finally succeeding, they dragged their craft onto the beach. Iakano knew their canoe was harder to handle because his presence made it overloaded, and from the curt way they treated him he sensed that the others shared that assessment.

"Let's explore as much as we can before we meet here for the night," they agreed and hid the canoe in the bushes. Each drank their fill with cupped hands from the small nearby stream and set out.

Iakano decided to go straight up the middle of the hillside. He climbed for some time, before sitting down to rest. He judged by the position of the sun and the grumbling of his stomach that it was late afternoon. He spotted a bush with edible berries further up the hillside, and reaching the generous bush, he satisfied his hunger. After filling his gourd pouch with berries, he noticed a ledge further up, and behind it a dark space, festooned with hanging ferns. He knew that signaled a cave, and decided to investigate. *Otherwise the preceding climb would have been a waste,* he reasoned. But by the time he reached the cave the sun had nearly set. So knowing that a descent to the beach was too precarious in the dark, he cleared an area behind a boulder, and peacefully fell asleep.

9
Meeting

Raisha's sleep was far from peaceful. She stirred at every small noise. She dreamed that the large, orange bird stood by her and peered at her with dark eyes. It scratched in the sand actually seeming to be trying to write something. Then a shuffling noise became too real and she woke up with a start. Her arm was numb from being pressed between her body and the hard ground. She stretched and her eyes followed a beam of daylight streaming into the cave.

What she saw at the cave's entrance froze all her movement except her wildly beating heart. At the cave entrance was the unmistakable silhouette of a man. She was sitting up by the time he saw her and there was no way to hide. Reasoning that appearing bold was her best defense, she got up and walked toward him. Even in her fear she was struck by the beauty of his physique, amply revealed by the scant native loincloth he wore.

"Aloha," she said trying to sound confident, but she could not suppress the quiver in her voice. "Hello," he replied with a smile.

Taken back at how the perfect pronunciation of the English word contrasted with his appearance, she quipped: "What is this, dress up day?" His hurt expression made her regret her flippant remark. "Look, I'm sorry if I offended you." She tried to add casually. "I am just waiting for the rest of my party and your appearance was well, unexpected." She saw him scanning the small path her descent to the cave had made, and realized that she had not fooled him.

"Please don't be frightened. I will not hurt you!" Her resolve started to buckle along with her knees. He managed to catch her, and prop her against the cave wall. "You look like you could use something to eat," he said and offered her the gourd filled with glistening berries. She looked at the berries, which were impossible to identify, crowded at they were and away from their stems. The thought that they might be poisonous briefly flickered across he mind, but then she took a handful. They were sweet and delicious and made her feel better. He sat cross-legged before her.

"What's your name?"

"Raisha, and yours?"

"Aisha.. That's a nice name. Mine is Iakano" *Aisha will do*, she thought. (The oddness of the situation seemed to be receding.)

"What are you doing here?" They both asked almost simultaneously.

He looked away toward the sea and Raisha decided she had better start. "I work at the Waioo Agricultural Station, and I came out here on an outing."

"Wow, I never would have picked you to be a farmer!"

"Not exactly. I am a scientist running a project to determine if pheromones could be used to lure insects off crops." (She sensed that he, unlike the field hands at the station, could comprehend this completely.)

"What are pheromones?"

"Hormones used by insects and other animals to send messages... often to attract mates." She blushed slightly at his raised eyebrows, and then tightened her lips, trying to look displeased. "So what's your story?"

"I live on an island to the north of here that was bought by someone very wealthy and given to the remnant of the native population with the stipulation that they would always retain their native culture and not let modern ways intrude." He said this in one breath, glad to get it all into one sentence.

"Is that even possible?"

"Well we have strict rules about venturing out."

"But how is it you speak fluent English?"

"I'll try to explain.... I was one who left the island and then was allowed to return."

"But why are you here?"

"I came here to find something..." Just then a loud call came from the beach below. Iakano was startled. "I must be going! Will you be all right?"

"Wait! I don't understand.... How did you get here? Are you by any chance that big, orange bird, changed into a prince?" Raisha was suddenly flustered.

He looked torn. "I will meet you here again..." Then he quickly sprinted down the slope.

She looked after him in disbelief. *Who is this guy? Does he think I live in this cave? There is no way I can stay here and wait to see him.*

Reluctantly she started the long trek back to modern civilization, following the path she took the day before.

10
An Old friend

Back in her small dormitory room Raisha collapsed on her bed after gulping down a sandwich she bought from a vending machine. She was asleep almost immediately. Visions of an exotic prince that morphed into a large orange bird pulsed in her dreams. She was awakened by a buzz, signaling that she had a phone call. (There were no phones in dorm rooms and one had to go to a phone down the hall).

"This is room 471. Is there a call for me?", she asked sleepily.

"Hi honey," a familiar voice said after a small click.

"Holy cow! Is the you Jack?... what...are you here?"

"How about some lunch? Better a picnic on the beach. Might as well live it up in this tropical paradise." Jack's voice was warm and enthusiastic.

Her thoughts jumped around as she hurriedly dressed. She was happy and excited about Jack's presence, but part of her longed to return to the green cliffs above a gently rolling sea and to a prince, somehow woven into that setting. Despite her haste, she was sure to adjust her hair and face to produce just the right impression of natural attractiveness.

Jack was sitting in the lounge downstairs, leafing through a magazine. His face lit up when he spotted her. "You look wonderful! Island life must agree with you." After a heartfelt hug, he tried to kiss her, but she turned her face. He paused awkwardly but said grinning: "How about you and me... getting hitched in a beach ceremony?"

Raisha rolled her eyes and grabbed his hand. "Lets go to get something to eat." They reminisced over old times and described their current situations. Raisha was impressed that Jack now worked in a large law firm in Washington, D.C., but through it all her mind was not with it. Finally she couldn't restrain herself any longer and plunged into the matter dominating her thoughts:

"Jack, you used to be interested in aboriginal island culture."

"Funny you should say that," he exclaimed, mildly curious. I have actually accumulated enough credits to minor in Anthropology."

Raisha scanned the horizon searching for a way to tell him what was on her mind. "I had the strangest encounter yesterday" she began slowly. "I went for a hike up Waikano Mountain and wound up spending the night in a cave overlooking a slope above a beautiful beach."

"You What !?" He interrupted.

"Well it was a deserted place... (She almost added, or so I thought, but Jack's frown stopped her.) "You know Jack,' she finally continued, "I'd like to learn more about the native culture here. There's a museum of that sort of thing near here. Let's go take a look." She got up and gathered the dishes on their table, hoping he wouldn't probe further.

He eyed her somewhat suspiciously, but said, "Good idea. I wanted to go there anyway." She sensed he wasn't satisfied and thought, *I shouldn't have said 'encounter'*.

The museum was a stone structure that used to be a post office. The surrounding vegetation gave the building an air of mystery. At the entrance sat a large woman wearing a colorful muumuu. She nodded smiling as Jack put some money into a donations jar. The interior was a contrast to the sunlit tropical garden outside. Jack started reading the historical explanations, while Raisha looked around hoping to find something resembling what she was beginning to fear had been just a dream. Then suddenly she spotted a large orange bird sculpture on a pedestal near the center of the room. "Jack!" she almost yelled and grasped his arm, pulling him toward the display.

"Wow," he said as they neared it. It measured about a foot and was covered with bright orange feathers, in exact and intricate patterns. "I heard of this bird deity. It was worshiped on these islands as the bringer of health and life. There are theories that it resembled an actual bird, which is now extinct." Raisha walked backward, keeping her eyes glued on the sculpture until she bumped into a stone bench and sat down. Images of the bird soaring majestically, and of a handsome smiling prince, flooded her mind.

"Just look at this exquisite craftsmanship," Jack exclaimed, absorbed in examining the bird-god sculpture. "You can hardly tell which feathers are real and which are carved out of wood. Do you realize, Raisha, that for this fine work they only had sharpened shell and bone tools?"

He looked around and saw that she was sitting on a bench behind him. "Are you all right?" he asked as he sat beside her, "You look pale."

"Let's go outside," she whispered. He took her arm as they walked to her car. "You better drive, Jack. I'm a bit shaky."

In the car he studied her face. "Maybe a good meal will do you good... and then you have to fill me in on your sudden obsession with native art."

"Forgive me, Jack. I guess I've been working too hard. Maybe I just need a good rest. Please take me back to my dorm."

"But honey," he complained, "I can only spend a couple of days here. I squeezed in this visit as a bonus of a trip I was taking to a conference in the Far East. I had hoped...." He stopped abruptly, but Raisha understood that he had hoped to rekindle their affair.

She begged off seeing him the next day, saying that she was coming down with something and Jack returned to the mainland. Raisha was not really sick but she felt unsettled. She never told anyone about the man she met at the cave above the pristine beach, or even about the amazing bird. She felt it was her wonderful secret. At other times she couldn't be sure that it wasn't all just a dream.

11
Resentment

Iakano was met by hostile stares when he arrived on the beach. The other three had already packed the canoe for a return trip to the homeland. Nothing was said, but he quickly understood the need for an early return: one of the companions had a badly injured foot.

At the village Iakano was shunned by nearly everyone. He sensed that his foray companions had complained about him, and spread a rumor that he may have had some renewed contact with newcomers. He was forced to go alone to the fishponds or to gather taro root. This was a departure from their customary socializing during these activities. What hurt him most was that he was forced to eat alone.

Only Alani's dark eyes followed him with sympathy. After a few days he was relieved to learn that the foot injury of his companion was healing well, and that a debriefing session about the last foray was finally scheduled. *At last I may be able to clear the air*, he thought. When the time came, the other three, from the foray, described where they went and then sadly admitted that they had not seen any signs the bird-god. Finally the leader of the month addressed Iakano: "Pease tell us what you did while on the big island." His tone was calm but the question seemed odd since the others were simply asked what they found.

All eyes riveted on Iakano as he stood and said: "I started up the middle of the hillside since the other ways were already taken. The climb was hard, and I began to consider abandoning it when I noticed that higher above there were hanging ferns indicating a cave. I felt compelled to investigate this, so I continued until the day was so far gone that I feared to climb down in the dark." He paused, weighing how much more to tell. "There was indeed a cave there. It looked like a possible home for Anara, though I did not see him or her." He added hastily, "I want to return as soon as possible."

There was an uncomfortable silence. All waited for some decision. Finally the leader said: "The forays are necessary and will continue. The time of the next one will be announced later. I do not know yet who should go, but I wish for Iakano not go go." Iakano's shoulders slumped, but he did not dare contradict him. The crowd sat for while mulling over his words. All thought that the leader knew best, for it was believed that he could commune with gods.

Later that evening Iakano sat in front of his hut weaving a pouch. When he glanced up from his work, he was surprised to see Alani. In her hand she held a tray with pieces of coconut and fruits arranged in a beautiful representation of a flower. "I didn't hear you, Alani. Please sit down." He motioned to a place next to him on a mat of woven grass.

She sat shyly, keeping a safe distance between them and handed him the tray of fruit. He accepted it, feeling awkward but pleased. She kept her eyes aimed at her feet and said softly, "Tell me that it's like on the other island."

12
Determination

Iakano had hoped that once the debriefing was done, all would return to normal, but most people still persisted in avoiding him. With no one to talk to, his loneliness began to consume him. He understood why they feared newcomers, because he had seen some thoughtless exploitation of the islands by various mainlanders.

He decided to try asking advice from a man who had been his closest friend, Keoko.

"Please help me understand what's goin on," said Iakano after a perfunctory greeting, as he poked his head into Keoko's hut. The friend appeared pained, but motioned him forward. Turning to his guest, now seated beside him, he said, "You know how much we fear the newcomers. Many are distrustful of you because they feel you aren't really one of us."

"You mean the three who were with me on the last foray," Iakano retorted.

Keoko threw up his hands, indicating that he was giving up. But after he looked at Iakano's anguished face, he softened and grasped his friend's shoulder. "I believe that you did not contact any newcomers, and in time others will come to believe this also."

Iakano pulled away. "There's nothing I need to be ashamed of!" Then he got up and left.

Convinced that any chance of his going on another official foray was gone, he started planning how he could go back there on his own. (He just could not let go of the possibility that the strange girl he had met might lead him to Anara.) He worked even more diligently on his canoe.

One night, not trusting his resolve to persist longer, he packed his, finished canoe and newly woven pouch with fruit, nuts and dried fish, and with some trepidation set out into the waves.

He paddled for about an hour, while the moon shone on the water. Its light began to dim with gathering clouds and the sea started to get rough. Wind made it difficult to control the canoe and then a pelting rain started. Huge droplets drummed loudly on the wood of the canoe and stung his face. At that point he was too far out to return. He wasn't sure which way the shore was anyway. He fought hard to control the canoe, while his long hair, soaked with rain and sea, flayed in the wind that howled around his ears. He could not see even inches before his face. The waves were so large that most of the time his paddle just smacked the air, and controlling the canoe became impossible. His body grew cold and his mind wandered. He prayed to Anara. The sacred bird seemed to swoop down and lift him, and he felt at peace.

Raisha moved mechanically through her job duties. Researching material about the ancient bird-god and about a private island to the north, absorbed all her free time. She found representations of the bird-god in several commercial accounts of the islands history, and considered the possibility that she had conjured up the image having seen it before. Still one thought remained clear in her mind: she was determined to return to that cave.

Whenever possible she made preparations. She purchased sturdy hiking boots and wore them daily to be sure they became comfortably broken in. The bulk of her next paycheck was spent on a wonderfully soft down sleeping bag that could be rolled up into a small packet. She went to the outdoor sports department at the local Sears store to see what else she might need for an overnight stay in the forest. It always amazed her that there was a Sears in this faraway place and she smiled at things for sale there that couldn't be found anywhere else in the world. She found some pretty earrings, dangling drops made of polished, brightly red seeds. She decided to buy a Swiss army knife. *Maybe I'll find some fruit to eat*, she thought, and her taste buds remembered the sweet berries offered her in the cave. At book outlets she asked about information about old island culture and searched out scholarly books about the topic in the college library.

Finally, having collected and identified all the insects in her traps bated with commercially bought pheromone-like chemicals, she renewed the whole setup, according to her experimental protocol, and felt justified in notifying her boss that she would be taking some time off. She was sure he would assume that she planned visiting the mainland.

Early next morning, she dressed for the outdoors and packed her backpack: nutrient bars, dried fruit, water bottles, a change of clothes, necessary toiletries and matches. She attached the compact sleeping bag to the bottom of her backpack. Her only weapon was the Swiss army knife in her pocket. She figured her provisions were adequate for at least who days. She slung a pair of binoculars around her neck and at the last minute put on her red seed earrings. They looked incongruous with her bulging backpack, but made her feel attractive and in touch with local nature. The walk to the outskirts of the town was uneventful. No one was around at that early hour. Looking up at the sky above the hills, still rosy from the sunrise and filled with wondrous cloud formations, remnants of a recent storm, she resolutely marched into the brush.

13
Two Souls

When Raisha arrived at the cave, the sky over the horizon was more beautiful that usual. Billowing clouds looked like a setting for some celestial revelation. Rain-cleansed air mingled perfectly with the perfume of flowers gleaming luxuriantly on some bushes. Her one disappointment was that there were no signs of any orange birds. She unpacked her gear and sat down at the edge of the hillside. With her binoculars she scanned the beach below, and suddenly she spotted something that made her stand and gasp: *My God, is that a dead man?*

She felt numb as she scurried down the steep slope, disregarding brambles catching the cuffs of her jeans and the occasional slips her boots made in the soil still damp from a recent rain. Reaching the man sprawled on the sand, she noticed to her relief, that he was breathing. She looked around but saw nothing to indicate how he got there. Then she heard him moan. His eyes flickered, and spotting her, he smiled.. She recognized the bird-prince of her dreams. Then her practical instincts took over: *I must get him out of the sun,* she thought resolutely. "Hello," she said trying to sound matter of fact, "Do you feel any pain?"

To her astonishment, Iakano sat up. "I was hoping to meet you here again!" His smile broadening as he looked into her eyes.

She looked away. "Ok, before I get to find out what you're all about, can you move over there into the shade?"

He got up with some difficulty, and with her help hobbled toward the green rim of the beach. Then he steered her to the left, explaining:

"There is a fresh water spring there."

After both quenched their thirst, Raisha wanted to ask a thousand questions, but then she saw him nodding his head. She knew that going up the steep slope would be harder than her frantic sprint down it, and that she had to start up right away to get supplies, mainly food. Looking at the now sleeping Iakano, she frowned in frustration at the lack of anything to cover him with. Finally she took off her shirt and pants, and used them to cover him as well as possible. Then she gathered some dried grass to further shelter his body. (She knew the nights got cold near the ocean.) As she climbed the bank, in her undies, she thought: *Thank God this area is deserted.* When she reached the cave she just managed to slip on her spare pants and shirt before she fell asleep in her sleeping bag.

She woke at the break of dawn, packed all the belongings she could assemble into the backpack and started on the precarious journey to the beach. Following the path she had trekked now twice was easier than she had remembered, especially when she abandoned all grace and slid down partly on her bottom. Still she had to rest several times to catch her breath. When she reached the beach, her heart sank, because the spot where she had left him was empty.

"Aisha!" He called to her from the surf.

"Hi," she waved enthusiastically.

"Come on in. The water's warm"

"Don't be absurd. We have to get something to eat and build up your strength."

"Yes ma'am." he said with a mock salute and sauntered out of the water, still in his birthday suit.

Raisha determined not to notice his nakedness, busied herself retrieving provisions from her backpack: two nutrient bars, apples and a canteen with water.

"Let me contribute to this breakfast," he said as he pulled a green leaf with some orange plums and red berries from the bushes. He noticed that she was trying to avert her eyes and he took the shirt she had left him the night before a deftly wrapped it around himself. It made him look like an Indian guru. After some minutes of munching and drinking from the canteen, he broke the silence: "Please tell me about yourself. I am so full of wonder. It is like being in a fairy tale."

She had to smile, thinking how accurately that described her own feeling. "My name is Raisha Endicott. I work at the Waioo Agricultural Station."

"Yes, I remember. You play around with sex." She gave him a stern look. Up till then she had been feeling aroused in a way that made her uneasy, but that remark worked like a cold shower. "I also remember that I was called away just as I was going to explain why I was here," he continued.

At last maybe I'll get some answers, she thought, her annoyance abating.

"Please start with how you came to be on the beach this time."

"You're right. This was hardly a conventional arrival. Well, maybe you remember that I live on an island to the north that was bought by someone very...."

"Yes, yes I know about that," she interrupted impatiently.

He looked out over the water.

"Before I continue, would you please answer a question that has been in my mind ever since our first meeting, because of something you said. You said you saw a large, orange bird!"

Her pulse quickened. "When I was here last I think I saw a big, orange bird.." Then after a pause, she added "in a dream."

35

He grasped both her hands and looked into her eyes. "I think it was a very significant dream." She knitted her brows. "I have to start at the beginning for you to understand?... He stood and started pacing, brushing back his long hair. Raisha pulled over the leaf with the fruit, and sat back against a palm tree. Popping berries into her mouth, she looked almost like someone waiting for a favorite movie to start. "Long ago, my people lived all over these islands. Their life was balanced with all the plants and animals around them. Then 'developers' (he said the word with a sneer) cut down our forests and polluted our water."

Raisha sighed, "So what else is new?"

"Unlike most native people, a small group of us was given a kind of reprieve: One of the rich 'developers' had a great deal of money and it seems also a guilty conscience, for he bought one small outer island and designated it to be our sacred land. He invited a remnant of us to live there undisturbed with only one caveat: that we would have no contact with newcomers or what he termed 'the modern world'".

"OK, I already knew that. When are you getting to why you are here?"

As I said, we have special relationships with animals, who share our life spirit. One of these animals is most important: Anara, the god of life itself. This spirit protects us and our health, and becomes visible to us as a beautiful orange bird."

"Our legends say that Anara's primary home is on this island. So when we stopped seeing his/her image (you see Anara can appear as either sex), we started sending out expeditions to try to find them." (She smiled thinking: *Nice... These people are less sexist than we are.*) "I had gone on one of these searches when I was young and became ensnared by the ways of newcomers, ... I mean in your ways." (Raisha became torn between resentment and sympathy.)

He took a deep breath. "I don't want to waste time explaining that phase of my life. Suffice to say that I decided to try getting back to our island." Then his narration became halting.... "It wasn't easy but eventually....my people did take me back... although...anyway I'm trying to determine for myself if the incarnate Anara spirit really lives here."

"OK, don't start getting all native on me, you seem much too civilized." *Why do I say such things*, she thought, and quickly added: "Actually I learned about this bird-god. Do think that's what I saw?"

Iakano said softly but resolutely, "Yes!"

How wonderful if I can be a part of this, she thought, and then said: "But all that doesn't explain how you wound up lying, half-conscious on this beach."

"Well..." he hesitated, "because my people are still very suspicious of me, I was not allowed to go on any future expedition. So I tried to canoe here by myself."

"...and was caught in a big storm." Raisha finished. Then she took his hand and said without hesitation: "I will help you look for this bird if I can."

"Lets go for a swim," Aikano threw off his make-shift cover. Startled, but laughing, Raisha pulled off her shirt and pants also, and after some hesitation even her underwear (not wanting to get it wet) and ran into the surf after him.

In the water Iakano led her to the edge of a reef and pointed to small brightly colored fishes nibbling iridescent seaweed in sparkling water. Then hand in hand the two nude, smiling humans made their way toward the shore. The surf swirled around her, but Aikano's firm grip made her feel safe.

"I'm hungry, are you?" He said as they stepped out of the water. She pulled away her hand, smoothed out her wet hair and ran toward their camp. There she used her shirt as a towel, put it on and rummaged through her backpack.

"Wouldn't you rather have some fresh fish? He asked as he squatted beside the provisions she laid out.

She stood, happy to see that her shirt was long enough. "OK, show me how to catch fish here."

He picked a straight branch from a nearby tree. "If only I had something to sharpen it with."

"Ah," Raisha said triumphantly, and whipped out the Swiss army knife." He took it beaming and deftly sharpened the end of the stick.

"Now I will need your help," he said. She threw off her clothes, which was easier this time (she only had on her long shirt), before she followed him into the surf. He led her to a cul-de-sac at the side of a cliff, pointed to a large silver fish and indicated that she should stand blocking its path off escape. Then he speared it deftly on its head so that it died instantly. After they brought it to their camp, he laid it on a large green leaf. "I'm going to look for some herbs. Maybe you can start a fire."

When he was gone she replaced the long shirt with her bra and panties, grateful that they were her favorite, the ones with a lace edging.

When he returned she was already stoking a fire using all her old Girl Scout skills and the matches she had brought. He eyed her approvingly as he gutted the fish, stuffed it with the herbs he had collected, and wrapped it in the green leaf.

"We will steam it as soon as the flames die down. You know you never told me why you came back to this place." Then seeing her blush, he added "I will be eternally grateful that you did." Raisha could only stir the glowing embers.

They ate the deliciously flavored fish in silence, and drank pure water from the stream. Then Raisha said what both had been thinking for a while: "Let's go up to the cave. We might spot the orange bird!"

Iakano nodded, doused out the fire and stored their provisions under a bush. He fashioned a loincloth from a large leaf and fastened it to a waist-band, made from a long plant fiber. "You better put on your pants and boots", he said casually and started up the slope. She finished dressing quickly, stuffed a couple of nutri-bars in her picket, hung her binoculars around her neck, and, fastened a canteen with water to her belt. *He may have some ingenious way of collecting water but I won't take any chances*, she thought. Then looking up toward their goal, she marveled at his agility and barefooted steadiness, to say nothing of his sexy bottom.

14
Confirmation

Iakano made the ascent easier by picking out the best footholds and clearing branches from Raisha's path. At the cave she flopped against a cool, moss-covered rock. The day was drawing to a close.

Just stay here and relax," said Iakano. I will prepare the supper meal." He went off into the woods. Raisha felt warm and happy. *What a great guy.* He returned shortly and asked to borrow her knife. Then he deftly peeled some roots and cut up fruit he had collected. They ate in a comfortable silence.

"It's late," Iakano said. Anara should not be disturbed at this time of day. We should get some sleep and look for them early in the morning." Raisha settled into her sleeping bag. She stole quick glances at Iakano as he made a bed out of leaves at the entrance of the cave. His presence there made her feel secure and she quickly fell asleep.

The next day, he woke her with another presentation of shoots and fruit. She sat up and reached for a small white root. "No wait," he called," That's for chewing after you eat. It cleans your teeth. He smiled broadly and she admired his strong white teeth. *I wondered now he keeps them so clean.*

With the morning sun barely starting to rise, Iakano stood at the edge of the canyon, cupped his hands around his mouth and produced a hauntingly beautiful sound. (Raisha remembered hearing it at this spot before.) She grabbed her binoculars and joined him in scanning the still dark sky. He repeated the call three times before a distinct echo reverberated through the canyon. They looked at each other in excited anticipation.

She was still looking into the trees when Iakano quietly laid his hand on her shoulder, made a sign with his finger to be quiet and pointed ahead. Directly before them flew a stunning large orange bird. His dark eyes seemed to be scanning them intently.

Suddenly there came another cry from the treetops and the magical bird flew off, its long tail feathers trailing gracefully behind him. Raisha and Iakano were so filled with wonder that they couldn't speak. Instead they fell into each other's arms.

They stood entwined for a long while. Nothing but joy and excitement pulsed through Raisha. Then she opened her eyes and moved to sit on a nearby rock. She drank from her canteen and offered it to Iakano. He accepted it and took a swallow.

At last Raisha spoke. "What are we going to do now?"

"We must offer the Anara family their favorite food and try to persuade them to come to live with us."

Raisha almost said something like "give me a break", but instead she said: "Getting their favorite food is a good idea. Can you gather it here?" Iakano nodded. "Good you do that, and I'll go back to the station and try to find an ornithologist and an anthropologist familiar with these islands. If we are lucky maybe both in one."

"NO! You can't tell any other newcomer about this!" Iakano said loudly.

She felt exasperated, but managed to control herself. "We must get some help! This is a very important discovery, finding something so rare. We have to try saving it."

He was troubled and sad, but after a while he said, "Let me go with you."

"OK, that may be good," she said with a smile looking at his tan muscles, but first I must bring you some ...er... covering."

14
An Ally

Back in her small office, Raisha opened her computer, where she found several messages from Jack. She scanned them, but didn't answer them. Instead she called up a list of the biology faculty. As she feared, most of them were specialized in molecular aspects of cells. At last she found some ecologists and read their biographies. She settled on a Dr. Edgar, who listed bird evolution among his interests. Her phone rang just as she was about to dial the phone. It was her boss, Dr. Verner.

"Raisha, I'm glad you're are back. There's been some trouble with my grant, and I urgently need to talk with you. Please come to my office right away!" He hung up before she could say anything.

Before obeying her boss's order, she dialed the ecologist's number and got a recording: "I am away from my desk, please leave your name and number and a brief message." She did so, saying only that she needed to speak to him urgently about a native bird.

Arriving at Dr. Verner's office, she was told that he was expecting her, and was offered a cup of coffee. "No thanks, I don't expect to be here long," she answered, pacing impatiently. The secretary looked at her curiously, and went back to her typing. After some minutes, Raisha asked the secretary for a piece of paper and pencil, and jotted down things she had to take care of: gather more provisions for the cave; get hold of Edgar or someone equivalent; possibly ask Jack for help. She was just about to force her mind to concerns about her pheromone experiments, when Verner stepped out of his office and motioned her to come in. He looked somber.

"Let me come directly to the point," he said after she sat in the chair he indicated in front of his desk. "We have lost the funding that includes your project. So you have only the time left in this semester, i.e. two months, to wrap things up. I am sorry. I know this is bad news. Please feel free to use my name as a reference."

He then turned his attention to papers on his desk, obviously indicating that he wanted her to leave. Raisha, filled with other dreams, simply nodded and walked out.

On the sidewalk she felt anxious but also relieved. She decided to go over to the biology building to try finding this Dr. Edgar in person. She asked some students at the building where she might find him, and they pointed to the courtyard: "He's probably tending his native plants," they said. Stepping into the courtyard was like stepping back into the forest, except that each area of the yard had a distinctive look: in one corner grew large Cycads and Bromeliads; another was filled with cacti, some of which were spectacularly displaying their annual blooms; various palms lined the walls; and in the center a pond held beautiful floating lilies. She almost forgot her quest by the time she stumbled on a white-haired man on his knees digging around some succulents.

"Dr. Edgar?"

He looked up smiling." Yes. Are you a new student?"

"I work at the Waioo station, with Dr. Verner. My name is Raisha Endicott."

"What do you do there? Surely they don't have you tilting the fields."

"I am a research scientist. My PhD is in chemical ecology."

"Well now, that gives us a lot to talk about," he said straightening up. "Did you really cover both chemistry and ecology? In this day and age, this may be the best approach. If you can't beat 'em join 'em, eh?"

"Dr. Edgar I would love to discuss all that with you, but right now I have a more urgent matter on my mind."

He looked at her intently, got up, took off his gardening gloves and steered her back into the building. In his cluttered office, he cleared a stack of reprints from a chair by his desk and offered her a cup of coffee, which she gratefully accepted.

"Now just relax and start at the beginning."

"I read that one of your interests is birds." He nodded. "What do you know about the native birds of these islands?"

"I consider all of the native biology here my primary interest."

Raisha moved to the edge of her chair, "Did you ever hear of Anara, the bird-god?"

He pulled a book from a shelf, opened it to a central page and presented her with a splendid painting of the bird-god.

"Its extinction is a tragedy," he sighed.

"What would you say" she asked breathlessly, "if I told you I saw one of these alive yesterday?"

He looked at her with a kind but pained expression. I'd say that you were dreaming. People haven't seen them for decades." Then he looked at his watch.

"Wait!" She almost grabbed his arm in fear that he would leave. "I hiked through the forest up Waikato Mountain. It took almost a whole day to reach the coast overlooking a small beach at the base of a cliff." Dr. Edgar settled back in his chair, he was willing to hear her out. She continued: "There I caught a glimpse of a large orange bird."

"Ah", he lifted his pointer finger, and leafed through the book again. He found a picture of another orange bird. It was interesting, but its beauty paled in comparison to the bird-god. "This no doubt is what you saw. It can still be found in the high mountains, although it too is now threatened."

"No, please let me finish. I also once thought that... that my glimpse might have been something else, but there is much more to my story. You see I met a man there." She blushed slightly and Dr. Edgar raised an eyebrow. "He came from that native island to the north. He was there trying to find Anara. Then with his help.... You see he can imitate their call... he called them in. It was amazing and so beautiful." She collapsed back into her chair, breathless.

Dr. Edgar scrutinized her, apparently weighing his options. At last he leaned forward and answered: "Look, there's nothing I would like better than to find the Anara bird alive. Why it would be the highlight of my career. But you have to supply me with some real proof before I devote myself to your cause." He opened a cabinet in his desk. "This is a good Polaroid camera that my last research student gave me. I'm sure you can figure out how to use it. Present me with a picture of this phenomenon, and I will do all I can to help you."

Raisha took the camera and thanked him. "I'll be back in a few days," she promised, and almost ran out of his office. She recalled that she had to collect insects from the traps and preserve them for analysis later. There's no need now to set up the traps again. I also have to buy clothes for Iakano, extra film and new provisions.

After accomplishing these tasks, she packed a new backpack (taking not only the bulky Polaroid but also her own 35 mm camera), grabbed a sandwich and set out for the cave.

15
Documentation

She reached her destination at dusk. Feeling drained physically but energized emotionally, she smiled as she noticed an elaborate feeding platform, attached to a nearby tree, laden with berries and greens. Iakano was sleeping stretched on her unfurled sleeping bag, just inside the cave. She gratefully joined him and fell asleep.

She woke just as the morning sun was creeping into the cave. Looking around for Iakano, she thought: *He has a way of always vanishing*. Then she spotted him outside working on the platform. "Hi, I have good news!" a professor at the university is willing to help us," she said as she approached him, happily.

She expected him to be happy too, but instead he said brusquely: "I thought I asked you to wait before you involve anyone else!"

"Be realistic. This is much too big for us to handle ourselves. Don't you think we need someone who really understands birds?"

"Understands birds! I see. To you this is just another biology project."

"Do you expect to reason with these creatures and have them follow you home just because you talk nice?"

The two would have gone on bickering if a gorgeous bird had not suddenly swooped down onto the platform. Raisha and Iakano watched it with awe, as it settled majestically, peered at them and then looked up into the trees as if to signal someone there.

Raisha rushed to retrieve her backpack and took out the Polaroid camera. She snapped a picture just as a second bird, just as spectacular as the first, though it lacked the gracefully trailing tail feathers, landed beside her mate. Then Raisha reached for her other camera and snapped several more pictures. She fumbled inside her backpack without taking her eyes off the winged pair, and mounted a telephoto lens. Having taken al least ten closeups from various angles, she ventured closer. The birds looked at her, but continued feeding. She switched off the bigger lens and finished the roll of the film. Then she took up the Polaroid camera again and exhausted its film, while the pair of birds poised obligingly. Iakano stood by reverently. Finally the winged visitors voiced a muted cry, which Iakano echoed, and they flew off. Raisha felt suspended. After a while she gathered the Polaroid snapshots scattered around her. The images were amazing. She thought: *I hope the close ups are even better.*

"I know that you are sincere about trying to help," Iakano said apologetically as he examined the Polaroids. "I'm sorry I lost my temper"

"And I apologize for belittling your obvious ability to communicate with them. Maybe we should stop arguing and plan what to do next."

They sat eating some greens and fruit. "Please, Iakano, come with me to meet Dr. Edgar. I promise we will not divulge the location of this cave." (She felt a pang of guilt when she remembered that she had already told the professor that she had hiked up Waikato Mountain.) Iakano nodded and she took his hand, trying to communicating that she understood his worries.

She took out the clothes she had brought for him.

"These have ample room so they are sure to fit you."

He straightened up: "I have to put some more food on the platform if I am to leave for a day or so."

"Are these all they eat?"

"Like most of us, they rely on fish too, which they capture themselves." Then he gingerly pulled on the shorts and tee shirt she brought.

"I refuse to wear these shoes," he said, tying on a pair of his newly woven grass sandals.

They arranged all their provisions in the back of the cave, replenished the platform with extra food, and started on their journey down the mountain. After walking for about an hour, they heard some laughing ahead. Both froze. Then Iakano deftly disguised the path they had taken. *Please let them not find the way*, Raisha prayed as they veered away from the unwelcome sound. Iakano steered a zig-zag path as they continued, so no one could easily find their footsteps.

16
Obstacles

In town she bought some fast food for both of them and checked Iakano into a cheap motel. (Luckily, she had a credit card.) She was nervous about spending money, remembering that her meager paychecks would cease in two months. She never considered spending the night at the motel herself. (The blinking neon sign and a motel smell dispelled any romantic notions.)

"I'll return in the morning. Right after I line up a meeting with Dr. Edgar."

She had to argue with the guard at her dormitory for it was past the curfew imposed on the residents there. "I had to complete my experiment," she offered, which was not far from the truth. *I am trying to accomplish something important here*, she assured herself.

In the morning she tried calling Dr. Edgar, but again heard only his canned message. So she recorded: "I have good news and will try to catch you today." She took the film from her 35 mm camera to a store that offered fast developing service, and rushed to Iakano, whom she imagined would be feeling nervous in his present surroundings. Her heart started to pound when there was no answer to her knocking on his door. She ran around to the back of the motel and to her relief found him sitting cross-legged on a small patch of greenery. He looked terribly uncomfortable, but he managed to smile when he saw her.

"Let's get something to eat." As soon as she said it, she realized how small her stack of cash was. "I've already eaten," she lied. "Would you like an Egg McMuffin. That is easy to eat on the run."

He was about to reply with something like "Yuck!", but instead, after seeing her flustered state, he cheerfully accepted.

The developed fotos were exquisite. Armed with that proof, they sought out Dr. Edgar at his office. It was a great letdown to learn that he was out of town for two days "I don't think I can bare it here for two days." lamented Iakano. "So I will return to the cave and wait there."

"Please I have to do something with you here. Let's go see my boss. He is a reasonable person and has interests in preserving the environment."

Iakano was very reluctant, but eventually succumbed to Raisha's insistence. When she called Dr. Verner she was surprised that he answered in person. For a few seconds, she was tongue-tied, and she said breathlessly: "Dr. Verner, may I come to your office right now to discuss something. I also want you to meet someone."

"Sure, Raisha," Verner said, sounding fatherly.

A sudden thought occurred to Raisha: Maybe he interpreted my timid tone to mean that I want to introduce a fiancée?"

When she walked into Dr. Verner's office with Iakano, she had to smile at the surprised look on Verner's face, and savored his temporary awkwardness. "This is Iakano. He and I need your help with something that could be of great importance to the preservation of native biology," she told him proudly.

Verner, now looking astonished, motioned them to sit down. He told the secretary to hold all calls and visits and then sat behind his desk. "Well now, please explain," he asked expectedly.

"As you probably know, Dr. Verner, there is a private island to the north which maintains native culture and forbids contact with the rest of the world." (He nodded.) "Iakano here is a member of the tribe that lives on that island."

"Well, Mr. Iakano, you must have decided to to leave it," Verner said with a smirk. Iakano lurched as if to leave, but Raisha grabbed his shirt and he sat down again.

"Take a look at these." She said and laid in front of him, a few of the photos she had just picked up. (She selected some that could not reveal the place where they were taken.)

Verner scanned them several times with growing intensity. "I believe this is the Anara bird that I have read about. Where were these taken?"

Iakano gave Raisha a forbidding look, and she said, trying to stay calm: "This bird is sacred to Iakano's people. They have been searching for it for a long time and now that we have found it we need a strategy on how to preserve it."

Verner, absorbed in his own thoughts, finally stated: "If this was taken on this island, it is just a matter of time before others discover it." Raisha thought of the hikers they heard on their way from the cave, and her mind filled with dread.

Iakano's eyes narrowed as he watched Dr Verner getting excited. "It is the wish of my people to transport Anara to our island." He said resolutely.

Verner countered condescendingly: "I doubt that can be done Mr. Iakano birds have minds of their own and wish to stay in their usual habitat. That's why the greatest danger to native species is destruction of such habitats. Let me call my friend, Dr. Edgar. He will be more able to advise..."

Raisha interrupted. "Fine, but don't bother now, he is out of town for two days. I have already spoken to him."

"I know someone in the local government, who may be able to steer us to the right office." Verner leafed through a Rolodex on his table.

Iakano stood. "Enough! I won't allow you people to take over!" Turning to Raisha, he said in an anguished voice, "I wish I had never met you!" Then he stormed out of the office. Raisha ran after him, and to the secretary's astonishment Dr. Verner quickly followed.

Iakano was out of sight by the time Verner caught up with Raisha, who having lost Iakano was slumped on a stone fence. "Looks like our native friend has a temper," Verner said panting. Raisha gave him a dirty look. He sat next to her. "I can see that that this is something important. And I want to help." He sounded sincere. "What do you need right now?
"I need a good meal," she said, weak from hunger and exertion.

"Let's go." He led her to the nearest restaurant. She gulped down a hamburger, blotted her mouth and said, "Please, Dr. Verner, I can't disclose the location. It would jeopardize Iakano's trust."

"OK, just tell me if it is on this island." Raisha looked out the window and knitted her brows.

"Hmm, Verner thought out loud: "Considering there's only one pristine and relatively inaccessible area here, it must be the east side of Waikano mountain." Raisha slumped in her seat, and hung her head. "Now, I think our best bet is to apply to the local government to get that area declared a nature preserve." He ignored her agitation. "It will be hard, because there are all kinds of developers around, chomping at the bit, and the locals are itching to get their hands on their money.... But having Dr. Edgar on board will help. You said that you already contacted him?"

"Yes", Raisha replied weakly, and then more firmly: "Right now I have to find Iakano.

"OK, I will discuss all this with Dr. Edgar as soon as I can. Will you let me have more photos to show him?" Raisha held her pocketbook with the pictures close to her chest. "Please, just give me some of the close-ups. She leafed through the pictures, and reluctantly selected a few of them. *Besides I have the negatives,* she thought. Still she looked at them lovingly before handing them over. In one Anara's tail feathers were ruffled by a breeze, and his powerful talons were curled around a golden fruit. As if posing, his dark eyes looked straight into the camera. Vernon took out his valet and placed five twenties on the table before her. "Take these you probably will need to buy some things."

17
Persuasion

Raisha bought food and more clothes for Iakano, and set out early for the forest. She was careful to make sure that no one followed her. *I wouldn't put it past Verner to have somehow spy on me,* she thought.

At the cave she found Iakano replenishing the feeding platform on which two magnificent birds were sitting with no apparent apprehension. She came closer. The birds looked up but did not budge. She absorbed some of the calm radiating from them.

"I'm sorry for running off like that," said Iakano. "I just felt overwhelmed." His eyes filled with tears when Raisha hugged him. "I can't stand having so many newcomers getting involved, and yet I don't know what else to do. I don't even have a way of getting home now since my canoe was lost in the storm."

"Listen to me," said Raisha, gathering all the resolve she could. "Dr. Verner suggested that we work to have this area designated a nature reserve. That seems to be the only way to accomplish saving the ..." (She was going to say birds, but did not want to offend.)

He sighed deeply, but then trying to sound hopeful he asked: "What would that involve?" "Well, it would mean getting the government..."

"Oh no!." He exclaimed and dropped his head into his hands.

She understood and shared his trepidations, for she had heard of political discussions about the environment that wound up favoring only those with money. Just then a relatively faint, but piercing sound echoed through the canyon. It made both of them gasp. The birds took off. "Was that a gun shot?," she asked breathlessly.

They looked at each other in panic. His posture seemed to collapse even further, but Raisha, in contrast, stood straighter. "Please come with me to talk again with Dr. Verner. We must discuss strategy." He made no further comment. Apparently comprehending that there was no time to waste, he dressed in the new clothes she had brought him, and even strapped on the new leather sandals. They walked back to town in silence. Iakano picked fruit along the way. The trees above were vibrant with bird life.

When she reached her office, in late afternoon, she immediately called Dr. Verner. His secretary said impatiently:

"Dr. Verner is busy and does not wish to be disturbed."

"Please, this is very important. Can you give him a message?"

"Not right now!" The secretary was clearly tired and annoyed.

"Please tell him Raisha and Iakano need to see him."

"He just started a meeting with Dr. Edgar and left instructions that no one should disturb them. So you had better try again tomorrow, I am about to go home."

Raisha hung up and grabbed Iakano's hand. "He's meeting with Dr. Edgar right now. I am sure it is about us. Let's go!"

They arrived at the administration building and found it already locked for the night. The window of Verner's office, however, was lit up. So they settled on the steps of the building, keeping their eyes on the window and on the only two cars parked in an adjacent lot. Finally the two professors came out walking energetically. Raisha and Iakano had to run to catch up with them.

"I didn't expect to see you so soon," Verner said sounding a bit annoyed when he spotted them "Here take some more money," and handed her another handful of bills. "I'll call you tomorrow."

Raisha accepted the money, knowing that she had to accommodate Iakano somewhere for the night. As Verner rushed into his car, she yelled: "Don't bother calling, we'll be back here first thing in the morning."

In a motel, she was just too tired to walk any further. They spent the night without any discussion.

In the morning they were told that Dr. Verner was not there. "No, I do not know when he will return", said the secretary. They waited for more than an hour, while the secretary avoided their glances. Raisha was uncomfortable, but Iakano was miserable. He took off his new sandals and rubbed his feet. Finally, Raisha suggested that they go to try seeing Dr. Edgar.

Dr. Edgar was just coming back from a lecture. He greeted them warmly and invited them in. "This must be our friend from the north island", he said extending his hand.

"Iakano." They both answered simultaneously.

Seated in Edgar's crowded office Raisha demanded. "Please tell us what is going on. We got the distinct impression that you and Dr. Verner were trying to avoid us."

"Oh, I'm sorry. Verner is anxious to get started on the negotiations.

"What negotiations?" Iakano broke in bruskly,

"Why Iakano I didn't expect you to be fluent in English." Then ignoring Iakano's annoyed face, he continued: "There is so much bureaucratic nonsense to deal with. We didn't think that you wanted to be involved."

Raisha swallowed hard. Her outrage made her tremble. "Didn't want to be involved! ...I now consider this my major focus and for Iakano it is a deeply held... (she considered how to put it)... cultural matter.

Iakano continued in the same tone: "We insist on being the deciding voices and must be included in all 'negotiations'". Then he turned to Raisha. "Have you revealed where we saw Anara?"

Raisha just knitted her brows and addressed Dr. Edgar: "Please explain exactly what is planned."

"Verner has connections at the capital. He is on his way there now to talk to someone about starting the paperwork to make the Waikano Mountain area a nature reserve."

At the mention of Waikano, Iakano stood, and reproached Raisha. "Who else have you revealed this to?"

She did not answer him but turned to Edgar. "Who will be in charge of the area? And what agency will be involved?'

Dr. Edgar only shrugged and said that he will keep them informed.

As they walked out, Raisha tried to sound reassuring. "I will go to any bureaucrats that get involved. Please don't worry. I don't think this is completely out of our hands. Mostly don't you agree that having the area declared a reserve is a good thing?"

Iakano was in a daze. He took solace in the native trees growing around the entrance of the building, with their branches silhouetted against a clear blue sky. Finally he said: "I am going back to the cave to guard Anara." She could find no words to reply.

18
A New Ally

Raisha decided to devote the next hours to sorting the insects collected in the last phase of her research. *At least I can get this out of the way and then I will have two reasons to seek out Verner,* she thought. Her nervous energy kept her at it the whole night.

In the morning the two field assistants found her slumped at her desk." Hi Raisha! If I were you I'd take it more easy. There's a beautiful day out there. Go and relax on the beach or something."

She sighed and smiled briefly. "Have you guys seen Dr. Verner around?"

"Nope not for a few days. Do you know what's up? We heard that you will be leaving? We'll miss you, you know."

"Thanks," she said and squeezed each of their hands "Do me a favor, please give this report to Dr. Verner when you see him and tell him that I need to talk with him right away." She handed them a copy of her research report thinking: *The more people trying to catch him the better.*

After the field assistants left she typed out a letter:

Dear Dr. Verner,

As I hope we made clear, when we first told you about our discovery, we only wish to do what is best for the native birds and their habitat. I am dedicating all of my time to this now. Please tell us (Iakano and me) of any undertakings you or Dr. Edgar are making in this regard.

I feel (and I am sure Iakano agrees) that your proposal to petition the powers that be, to have the area become a nature refuge is a good one. However, please understand that this is more than just a conservation project for Iakano. It is a deeply held religious matter in his culture and we must not disregard the native sensitivities. Accordingly I insist that we be appraised of what is going on and that Iakano and I will always be part of any future moves and decisions.

She read the letter over and was not quite satisfied, but she was too tired to revise it. So she sent it off as an email and printed several hard copies of it. Then along with another copy of her final experimental results, she carried all to Verner's office, where she told the secretary to give them to him ASAP and to please ask Verner to contact her on her cell phone when he comes in.

Sitting in the cafeteria she could not bring herself to just sit and wait. She considered going to the cave, *but without any plan, what can I accomplish there?* Then she thought of Jack. Glancing at her watch, she calculated that it was about 10 P.M. on the US East Coast, and she dialed Jack's number.

He answered after a few rings. "I was almost ready to give up on you", he exclaimed. "Please tell me that you have decided that marrying me is what you want!"

"Oh Jack, I have a situation here and there is no one to talk to."

"You're in luck, kiddo! I have two weeks vacation pending, give me a day to make arrangements and I'll join you in your tropical paradise."

Her eyes welled up with tears. "I didn't mean for you to...."

"Honestly, I think this is a great idea, please just hang on until I get there."

"Jack wait.... At least let me give you an idea of what's going on."

"OK, honey I'm listening."

She hesitated, trying to decide how to start. "Well... a friend of mine, who is native here... he and I have found a bird that was thought by everyone to be extinct. This bird is amazing... well you know about it, it is that Anara bird-god."

"Are you serious?"

"You know how things like this can develop - a couple of the professors here have... well sort of taken over. I agree with their suggestion that a nature reserve should be set up to protect this bird, but they have been so....so pushy. They seem to be actually ignoring me. They probably think I can't handle this. It's so upsetting because I feel it is MY cause. And, Iakano, that's my native friend, is very upset with me for having brought the profs into it. I just don't know what to do."

"My law degree might come in handy, in this! I'll look up environmental laws and take some relevant reading on the plane."

"I don't know what to say."

"Just say that you'll be glad to see me."

19
Roots

When Iakano arrived at the cave, he once again replenished the platform with Anara's favorite foods and ate some of them himself. Then he hurried to the beach below because he felt a need to bathe in the ocean. After his swim, which relaxed him somewhat, he went to the fresh water stream to rinse. When he reached it his stomach knotted again, for nearby he found a canoe, that told him a new party from his home was present. *I should have known that the bird calls were too numerous. Have I been away so long that I don't recognize them as human imitations?* he thought, as he washed, dressed and sat down to wait.

He was elated about the impending renewed contact with his people, but also he dreaded their probable reproaches about his venturing out on his own. He considered taking off his newcomer clothes, but then decided to face the music. He was never one to hide things.

After a while the search party appeared at a distance and Iakano happily noted that one of them was his old friend Keoko.

"Can that be you Iakano?, exclaimed Keoko. "We all thought you were dead!" He ran over, hugged him, and then drew back having touched his clothes. "We can't wait for you to tell us what happened." The others just stared at him.

Keoko said: "Why don't we cook our fish. Then we will have time for all our talk." They steamed the fish they had just caught, in their style and sat down around the dying fire. Iakano especially appreciated the meal, after all the fast food he recently had. He pondered how to best narrate.

"Please let me finish my whole story before you say anything," he said when they passed around gourds with various fruits. "As I told everyone before at the last foray debriefing, I climbed up this slope…" (He gestured toward it.) "and I wanted to examine a cave that looked like a likely home for Anara." He paused and swallowed, "What I didn't not tell at the debriefing is that I found a newcomer female asleep in that cave."

His audience gasped.

"Yes.... she was young and frightened, but after a while I managed to calm her down. We didn't get a chance to talk much at that time, but she did say something I couldn't forget: She said that she had seen a beautiful orange bird." (Keoko and his companions leaned closer.) Iakano, wiped his face and moved his hands in a gesture indicating things disappearing. "Then we had to leave the island and as you know most people were...(he searched for a right word).. unfriendly. All of it just made me...(he started to stammer),...no one seemed... to care."

"You know, Iakano, you are wrong. Everyone was broken up when we found pieces of your canoe. Alani cried for weeks." Iakano's eyes widened. He stood and strolled toward the surf.

Returning he resumed: "I now need to tell you the most important part of my story! I met this newcomer female again after I was washed up on this shore, and now she and I have indeed seen Anara!" (Their eyes widened.) "This newcomer woman and I have become friends. We are trying make this area a nature reserve." (They appeared bewildered.) "What that means is that we are trying to save the whole area; to make sure no newcomers are allowed to build here. There would be people in charge of keeping all the plants and animals here safe."

Keoko broke the long silence that followed. "You must come back with us, and tell this to everyone."

Iakano shook his head."I must stay here to help nourish Anara, and to learn what my friend (her name is Aisha) finds out and what we should do next. Do you think the elders will look kindly on all this?"

Keoko put his arm around his friend. "I'll do all I can to explain it to our people."

Aikano asked softly, "Was Alani really distressed?"

"I'm sure she will be relieved to learn that you are alive."

"Would you please tell her that I miss her and hope to see her again someday?"

Keoko nodded. "We will leave tomorrow, but first we want to see that cave."

Despite repeated efforts, Raisha could not get and "audience" with Dr. Verner, and Dr. Edgar could only tell her that he had not heard any news. She tried looking up the structure of the local government, thinking she might be able to go herself to some appropriate office, but the meager law library at the college had only outdated books. She even tried calling the numbers in the government section of the phone book, but none of her calls reached any live people, and her messages were never returned. Only the knowledge that Jack would be arriving soon sustained her.

On the day of his planned arrival, she drove using the research station's car, to the local airport. She bought a flower lei from a vendor. The terminal was small and resembled an outdoor market. There was only a roof with no walls. Arrival "gates" were actually fences separating the terminal with its baggage counter and ticket desk from the space where the airplanes landed. The runways were nevertheless modern to accommodate some jets that had lately started delivering a steady stream of tourists. When Jack's plane landed she stood on tiptoes to look over the heads of a crowd that had gathered.

"Hi beautiful !' Jack hugged her as she draped the lei around his neck. He noted her twisted face and grabbed her shoulders. "Now look we will get this done and being despondent is not like you. I'll show you how to fight City Hall!" She sat down on a bench near the baggage return and looked almost as if she might start to sob, "Wow, said Jack, "I think we should first go for a drink."

"I don't want to go to a bar. Let's just get you checked into some motel."

During the short drive to a motel, both were uncharacteristically silent. After he checked in, they went to a small coffee shop, decorated with large potted tropical plants and a small fountain. Raisha relaxed a bit and said: "For the past week I've had nothing but frustrations. I can't get anyone to speak to me, not even my current boss. An older biologist, a Dr. Edgar, who is an expert on native biota, seems like a good guy, but he claims to be in the dark as much as I am. Trying to get anything from the government is like trying to topple a stone wall."

"I have already telephoned the local 'Office of Environment Management'", he said brightly.

"I should have inquired about such a thing," she replied hopefully.

"It's a new department," he continued, "and they seem to be open to suggestions. I made an appointment for today already. Are you up to coming along?"

"I wouldn't miss it for the world!" Her tension was replace by nervous energy.

20

Common Cause

Feeling hopeful, Raisha drove to her dorm, took a quick shower, put on her white shift dress, and fixed her hair and makeup.

When she pulled up to Jack's motel, he was standing in the front, waving. He looked very professional in a light suit, holding an attache case. His boyish looks actually enhanced that image. The local city hall was a surprisingly elegant building, designed to resemble a volcano. It featured a courtyard ornamented by a large bubbling central fountain. They were directed to the "Office of Environment Management" by the clerk at the information desk, who had to look it up in his computer. "That's a new one for me," he said smiling.

That office was the last one down a long hall. Its door looked official, but inside they were shocked to find only a tiny space occupied by one desk and a few chairs. A man, who looked around thirty years old, was in the process of tacking a large Serra Club poster on the wall.

Jack asked, "Is this the "Office…"

"You must be Jack Soltano" interrupted the young official, and who is this lovely lady?"

"This is Dr. Raisha Endicott, who works in the experimental field station here."

The official motioned them to sit down "What can I do for you?"

Jack indicated deferring to Raisha, who started: "We have made a momentous discovery: We found a very valuable species, one that was believed to be extinct, and one that is sacred to the native population. It is a large and beautiful bird. Such a discovery is of great importance to all biologists, conservationists and evolutionists, as well as to cultural anthropologists."

She paused. The young official eyed her suspiciously. "Just what do you want our role to be in this?"

"We have consulted with professors at the University and concluded that to preserve this discovery we must preserve the environment in which, this 'living fossil' is found. It is one of the few pristine areas still left on this island. What we need from you is to help us designate it as a protected nature reserve."

"That must be Waikano Mountain", the young man sighed. "I'll try to help. But I have learned, in my short time here that making money is a much higher priority in our government than preserving either natural or cultural treasures." They exchanged pained looks. "There is a meeting in a week, which I helped plan, to air anyone's 'Environmental Grievances'. I will place you on the agenda."

"Both of us, and maybe also a representative of the native population, will definitely attend. We would like to make a formal presentation," answered Jack.

The official agreed to make a projections screen available. "Please realize that I am just about the lowest man on this power totem pole here, and I can't guarantee how much of a hearing the board will give you."

When they left the office, Jack said enthusiastically "We will prepare a presentation to wow them. Can you get this Dr. Edgar to come along? He would be a valuable asset."

"OK, I'll ask him. What about Iakano?"

"I think it's time I met this Iakano, who you seem so fond of."

"Yes," replied Raisha. "Let's both go to the cave. You have to see what I am talking about."

They shopped for some jeans and a sleeping bag for Jack. Raisha advised him to buy hiking boots, and to start wearing them right away. "It's important to break such shoes in. We have several hours of walking to do. She tried to contact Dr. Edgar, but was told that he was out of town, so she left her cell phone number and a message that she urgently needed to speak to him.

"You amaze me," Jack said as he watched her packing provisions into backpacks.

Jack brought along a video camera.

The next day during their trek through the forest, Raisha pointed out small inconspicuous clues indicating the way: a broken branch in an overhead tree; an area naturally clear of underbrush; a large rock; a small spring; or a moss-covered boulder. But she was always careful not to leave any obvious indications of where they walked.

After a couple of hours they arrived at a spot where the vegetation parted to show a view of her now familiar beach. "Wow," he said loudly this is even more beautiful than I had imagined."

"Raisha searched the view with her binoculars. Shhhh!" She hissed. "I see there is a canoe in the bushes down there." (That she could spot it was another testament to her growing abilities.) "That means there is a new search party from the north island here. I'm not sure how Iakano has reacted. We must go to him right away." Jack groaned, being exhausted, but got up immediately.

When the new foray from the small island reached the cave, they agreed with Iakano that the site looked like a perfect home for Anara. They prayed, and prepared to spend the night. Iakano was relieved that there was no sign of Raisha, because he wasn't sure how his friends would react to her.

He left the cave to look for roots and leaves to supplement their fruit supper. "I've lived here long enough to know where to find them," he assured the others. Some distance away he knelt to dig out young shoots of bamboo, when he heard the sound of footsteps. He hid behind a tree, but immediately stepped out when he saw Raisha. Then he startled when he spotted Jack, stumbling behind her.

"You must be Iakano," Jack said and offered his hand.

Raisha, for a minute at a loss for words finally said. "Iakano, this is my friend Jack. He is a lawyer. I know he will be a great help."

Iakano frowned. "What are you planning and how many more have you involved?" , he reproached Raisha.

She tried to speak, but suddenly started to feel faint. (She had had very little rest in the past days.) Iakano took her arm and helped her to sit on a log. Then he picked some berries from a nearby bush and offered them to her on his hand. She accepted them with a smile. Jack watched the silent ritual somewhat puzzled. Finally he sat down next to Raisha. Keeping her eyes on Iakano, Raisha said: "Jack is old classmate of mine. He has already made contact for us with the local government."

Jack added, addressing Iakano: "There is a trend in politics that may pay off for us. Especially if you can beef up the cultural angle."

Distrust filled Iakano's heart. He was about to respond when he heard Keoko and his friends moving toward them. Their native garb contrasted with Raisha's and Jack's hiking gear.

The new three mirrored Iakano's previous look of distrust. The tensely charged atmosphere almost made Raisha tremble...... when a large orange bird glided into view. It seemed to clear the air with a series of flaps of his powerful wings. Then he settled between the two groups. Everyone held their breath. The natives sank to their knees and the newcomers followed. The bird seemed to look around as if asking, "Are you going to help me?"

At last Iakano stood and addressed his compatriots in a calm voice: "My friend Aisha has returned. Please come and meet her."

Jack too recovered and started working his video camera.

"Please don't be frightened," Iakano said to the three natives, noting their wary looks."

"What is that evil looking eye he is pointing at Anara?"

"It makes pictures. Look Anara approves!" The gorgeous bird spread its wings once more and nodded his head in a display. Jack became so excited he nearly dropped the camera, but instead he dropped once again to his knees, getting some unbelievable close-ups.

Eventually Anara flew toward the cave area. The four natives followed the bird-god solemnly. Iakano looked back at Raisha and Jack to invite them to come along, and so they did. They all made a strange procession, led by the sacred bird.

Jack continued filming, ending the sequence with Anara's meeting his mate on the feeding platform, and capped it all with views of the beach and ocean below bordered with lush vegetation.

In the cave the three natives and the others sat on opposite sides. Iakano handed each person a large leaf with the edible things he had gathered. After they ate, he asked: "Please Aisha tell us slowly why it would be good to make this area a nature reserve. I will translate as you go."

Raisha stepped in front of the three from the north island. With Iakano at her side, her nervousness eased. Outside a cry from Anara could be heard. "I am happy to be able to talk to you." She paused for Iakano's translation... "We know how much.....we think we understand how much Anara means to you." (Some of the visitors smiled.) "Please believe me that we want what is best for Anara. .... We hope to protect this area, so Anara's family will always live here and prosper."

One of the three asked a question, which Iakano translated: "Will we be able to come here to visit Anara?"

"Yes, I am sure that will be arranged. We'll always keep this part of the sanctuary free of the tourists"

"What?", exclaimed Iakano, "You never mentioned tourists!"

"Well, I know that nature sanctuaries always make part of their revenue from teaching and tourism," said Raisha defensively... "We would work out details later."

The three sensed that they were having some sort of dispute. Their leader spoke to Iakano who tried to explain. All then went to the edge of the hillside overlooking the ocean, and Iakano told Raisha: "I think they understand."

In the morning, after the Anara pair once again visited the feeding platform, the three natives set out to return to their island, promising to try convincing everyone that the plan to preserve the area was best for Anara.

Raisha earnestly pleaded with Iakano to return to town with them. "It is very important, for you to attest to the authenticity of this project." He, somewhat reluctantly, agreed.

21
Bored Board

Raisha and Jack walked behind Iakano, who steered them carefully around some newly sprouted mushrooms, and pointed out small ant nests that looked like mounds of dirt, emphasizing that all must not be disturbed. Gently clearing branches in their way, he always carefully returned them to their place.

"As they neared the town, Raisha asked Jack discreetly: "Would you be willing to share your motel room with Iakano at least until after our presentation?"

"Sure Raisha. Maybe that way I will get to know this mysterious guy better.... We will arrange appropriate pictures on my computer to supplement our presentation talk." She was grateful to have at least one worry off her mind.

She tried to reassure Iakano: "I will see you in the morning. The presentation is now scheduled for tomorrow afternoon. It is important for Jack to fill you in on what we will say. We plan to call you to verify the concerns of your people." He nodded but remained uncomfortable.

She turned to Jack and whispered: Please be gentle with him."

He smirked: "Don't worry, I don't bite."

At night in her dorm room, she went over her speech many times. Then in her dreams she pictured the board members alternately as dimwitted apes or hungry lions. The next day she called Jack on his cell phone. "How are you and Iakano getting along?"

"He's been up for hours, sitting outside. I think he got up to watch the sunrise. As for me I am anxious to go. Let's go fro get something to eat."

"I can't, right now. I want to line up Dr. Edgar."

"OK, we'll meet you at the presentation."

She dressed quickly and got a pancake for breakfast in the dorm dining room. She rolled it up and ate it on her way to Edgar's office. His secretary still didn't know his whereabouts.. Raisha was beginning to think that he too was now trying to avoid her. She asked for a piece of paper and wrote him a note:

Dear Dr. Edgar,

Because you told me of your deep commitment to conservation of native biota, I am sure you will want to join Iakano, my native friend, and another friend, who is a lawyer, at a presentation we will make at an Environmental Grievances Board meeting at City Hall today. It will start at about 1 P.M at the City Hall We intend to plead for the creation of a nature reserve on Waikano Mountain, as you and Dr. Verner, had suggested We would be very grateful if you would come to add your valuable expertise.

I apologize for this short notice, but I couldn't get in touch with you before."

Sincerely,
Raisha Endicott.

She added her cell phone number and handed the paper to the secretary, who placed it in the middle of Dr. Edgar's desk.

At the City Hall, she noticed Iakano was looking unhappy as usual in shorts and a shirt. He was still carrying his sandals. Jack looked handsome in a Seersucker suit, and polished shoes. "You look amazingly relaxed," she said to him.

"It's a pose you learn in law school", he answered.

The conference room was about half filled and smelled of smoke despite the now years-long ban on smoking there. Several men, seated in front at a long table, were looking over some papers. The young man from the Environmental Management Office hurried over. "You are scheduled to be the third presenters," he said and motioned them to seats at the side of the room.

The first presentation dealt with sewage leaking from a large hotel by the beach. Raisha listened with dismay, bordering on horror, as the chairman deferred decision on the matter to another committee.

The second was a proposal for building a new hotel. Raisha became saturated into indifference with the overblown claims of how good for the local economy this hotel would be, when she was jolted to attention because she heard that the proposed site was Waikano Mountain.

"This area is totally undeveloped" continued the presenter with a grin. "Its untapped economic potential is enormous! We estimate the project could generate over five hundred jobs during the construction and then many more permanent jobs connected with the hotel and other tourist services once it is built. We don't have to tell you that tourism is our biggest industry."

Everyone in the room smiled and nodded. Raisha, Jack and Iakano looked at each other in desperation. Raisha's thoughts were racing. She didn't even hear the rest of that developer's presentation, but she was snapped to attention when the chairman said: "Dr. Endicott, are you presenting then next petition?"

She stood, squared her shoulders. Iakano, admiring her courage, was reminded of their first meeting.

"I'd like to present an overview first, and then call upon Iakano, a representative of the interests of endogenous peoples, to comment." She took a deep breath and fired up her first slide, which showed a long view of the area near their cave.

"It is indeed true, as the previous speaker said, that Waikato Mountain is 'undeveloped', by our standards. (She couldn't refrain from pronouncing the word with an air of derision.) The area is indeed one of the few left in our world that still houses much native flora and fauna, plants and animals that have disappeared, because of modern 'development', almost everywhere else."

The developer raised his hand and was recognized by the chair. "I actually agree with the story this you lady is showing. I ask you what could be wrong with having a pristine white tower, the hotel we are planning, in the middle oft this beautiful scenery. In fact, it is exactly this scenery that draws tourists. Our hotel would be an economic bonanza."

"I'll tell you what your 'pristine tower' would do," she answered. "First there would be the building phase, requiring huge machinery, which, in turn, would require new roads. Please try to image the pollution and noise that would generate. And later ...what about all the sewage all those many tourists would generate? (Just recall the first presentation we heard here today.) We want to highlight one specific bird found only in this area. It was driven from the rest of the island for those very reasons."

Jack stood to set up his laptop computer. He projected a distant view of the area, planing to follow it with a video of Anara taking off from their feeding platform. "Please dim the lights," he asked.

The developer, squirming in his seat, took advantage of the pause. "Mr. Chairman, do we really have time for this kind of theatrics?" I could have brought with me equally impressive pictures of our proposal."

A member of the audience called out "Let her continue!" Then another yelled: "Let's move on to other things. We haven't got all day." The chairman banged his gavel trying to quell the din, and then a strange sound filled the room. It was Iakano standing with arms raised, and chanting. His prayer quieted the commotion. it took a few minutes for the room to recover.

Raisha tried to continued making a case for the establishment of a nature preserve: "Something irretrievable will disappear, if we don't act" she pleaded. But no one was in the mood for more discussions.

The chairman simply said that Dr. Endicott's request will be taken under advisement, and gaveled the meeting to a close.

22
Nadir

Raisha, Iakano and Jack walked out of the capital building feeling drained. All three sat down in silence on a bench in a park across the street. A nearby vendor was selling oriental food and Jack went over to buy three egg rolls. (They hadn't eaten since early that morning.) Almost in spite of herself, the delicious smell of the hot food made Raisha feel hunger and she accepted one of the rolls. Some of the sauce from the roll squirted onto her white dress. This triggered a flood of emotion. Jack tried to wipe the stain from her chest and said consolingly: "I'll buy you a new dress, please don't cry." She leaned into him sobbing, and he added: "We'll get one this afternoon."

Iakano looked away. Concentrating on the strong roots of a tree encircling the bench they were sitting on, he whispered, "I must leave here."

Just then the young environmental officer came running toward them. "I'm so glad I caught up with you," he panted, out of breath. "I want to present your case at the next meeting of the Serra Club."

Only Jack could speak calmly: "Of course, just give me the time and place," he said, and then took the officer to the side to write down these details.

Raisha, now recovered, turned to Aikano: "Please believe that we will continue to fight to get this right."

He responded sadly. "Come with me Aisha...get away from this madness."

"I won't just give up!"

"OK, then you'll find me at the cave - I am willing to help if I can."

I wish there was some way I could reach him quickly, Raisha thought as she fingered her cell phone in her pocket. Jack was just shaking the officer's hand when he noticed Iakano walking away. He yelled: "Stop! We need him. Where is he going?"

"Let him go, Jack. He needs to return to the cave.. I can get him again when we need him." Her cell signaled before Jack could reply. (She had put it on buzz to avoid interruption during their meeting,)

"This is Edgar. Would you and Iakano come to my office this afternoon?"

"I will be there, but Iakano is currently unavailable. May I bring with me a good friend who has been helping us now?"

"Good I'll see you at two."

Dr. Edgar looked drawn and tired, but he greeted them warmly. "Let's go outside into the courtyard. I always feel better there." They sat around a table, which Edgar had to clear of dirt, flats and pots, left there by a sloppy student. Bird songs and flickering sunlight filtered through a large tree-fern above them. "Here's what's been going on: Jim..er.. I mean Dr. Verner went to see some powerful friends in Washington last week.... I thought that it was to discuss getting the Waikano area designated a nature reserve."

"Why haven't you told us this earlier?" Asked Raisha.

"I apologize....but well... nothing was certain and Jim, er Verner seemed to feel we should wait until things were real. Anyway now he is back and told me the details of the deal, which he is sure will go through." Raisha and Jack were at the edge of their seats. Dr. Edgar continued sounding worried. "The upshot is that we will get the designation at the national level, but only if we allow a considerable amount of commercial development."

"Like what?" Asked Raisha and Jack, simultaneously.

Well, there would be a lodge and roads and even a train service to the cliff. These were concessions to the developers who were busy lobbying the same committee that Verner was dealing with. Now Verner is enthusiastic, but I just can't support this particular plan! I know how vulnerable such a remarkably preserved area is. Do you two have some other ideas?"

Raisha sighed sadly, but Jack looked around searchingly, and finally said: "Maybe we can succeed in modifying the plans. We have to pull together all that we have. First the unique biology. We'll need you two to support the biology. We have some amazing photos and videos for that."

"Videos? jumped in the old professor, "I'd love to see them!"

As if not hearing him, Jack continued: "Then the ethnic angle… Preserving the ancient culture. I have some expertise in that." He turned to Raisha -" You have to get Iakano back." Then addressing the professor again he said, "There is a new meeting to be, with the local Serra Club. Will you join us Dr. Edgar? (Edgar nodded.)

"Meanwhile I'll contact the local newspapers."

"And I'll contact my colleagues. I know they will be supportive," added Edgar.

"What should I do?" Raisha asked, feeling somewhat left out.

"Go to Iakano and line up what you can from him," ordered Jack. Then he handed both of them a note listing the time and place of the Serra Club meeting. They shook hands and each rushed off, powered and with a new sense of mission. Raisha bought some supplies and laid down to rest in anticipation of an early morning trek to the cave.

23
Ad Hoc Forum

As Iakano walked toward the cave, his head buzzed with images of dirty sidewalks, noisy machines and polluted air. These faded as he absorbed the forest with all of his senses: The feel of moss and dried leaves under his bare feet; the soft hum of branches moving above with gentle breezes; the orchestra of various bird calls; and a clean smell of plants, animals and microbes living in balance. By the time he reached his destination it was already dark. He had eaten fruits picking them along the way. So he unrolled Aisha's sleeping bag, and feeling drained, fell asleep.

The midday sun was already drenching his sleeping area, when he was awakened by a familiar voice: "Iakano! Thank gods you are here!" It was his friend Keoko, followed by seven others from the island. Iakano sat up startled to see such a large group. "We are here to ask you to come back with us to talk to all our people."

"What happened?" Exclaimed Iakano, as they all sat in a circle before the cave. (He was puzzled for this was unlike the ways of their island.)

"Our people need more convincing; we just can't give them all the answers ourselves."

"I wish my good friend, Aisha were here," said Iakano. The others frowned, but he lifted his hand to stop their objections, "I have come to believe," he said in a firm voice. "That she and her friends and their plans are good for us."

At that moment Raisha scrambled down a path toward the cave. She scanned the unexpected group and went to Iakano. They greeted each other with a hug. The circle remained silent and intent. Iakano was somewhat embarrassed but pleased. "Look my wish was heard, for here she is." He swept his left arm in a presenting gesture, while holding his right arm around her shoulders. Then turning to her," he said: "They came to find out about the plan. Please explain it."

He kept his arm around her, for he sensed her nervousness. She looked at all the faces staring at her intently, it was very different from the reception she had received at the Environmental Board Meeting. "Well," she said, "We need to get the authorities to designate this whole area a wildlife refuge." Iakano translated as well as he could and a discussion ensued.

Finally Iakano said to her, "I had a hard time making them understand what a wildlife refuge means, but it finally sank in when I explained that it would mean that no newcomers would be allowed here."

"No, wait that's not right!" Raisha exclaimed.

Iakano nodded. " I see now. Give me a moment to try again...I'll tell them that some newcomers would be good." Raisha sighed and sat down on a rock. The discussion continued, long and heated. Finally Iakano turned to her again: "They want to know who are the authorities that have to be convinced."

"Good question," whispered Raisha. "We are not sure ourselves at this point. But we are working on it. Please believe me that we will not let it get out of our hands." (When she made that last point, she bit her lip.)

After some further explanations and discussions all agreed to do all they can to make the vision of a nature reserve a reality.

Iakano's seven neighbors returned to their island, but Iakano stayed with Raisha. The two sat at the edge of the cliff watching the sunset. There was a strained tension between them, and Iakano asked gingerly, "Who is this Jack, and what does he mean to you?"

Surprised by his question, she nevertheless felt she had to answer: "He was an important part of my life when we were students."

"...and now? persisted Iakano"

Now, I don't know," she answered honestly.

24
Serra Club

Raisha joined Jack at the motel where he was preparing for the Serra Club meeting, to be held that evening. He was on the phone all afternoon, trying to line up press coverage, but the only firm promise he could get was from the local College Newspaper. (People at the other papers thanked him, but remained noncommittal.) Raisha was happy to report that Iakano and his friends, who pretty much represented the entire north island, seemed supportive. "But I couldn't persuade Iakano to come back with me. He wanted to stay near Anara."

She rehearsed introductory statements she was to make, which were designed to set the scene. She was making up her face and hair, when her cell phone rang. It was Dr. Edgar. "I've lined up two of my colleagues, one from anthropology and another is an emeritus professor of botany."

"That's great, Dr. Edgar. We are planning to open with some stills of the area and the bird. Then we hope to have you explain the relevant ecology. Jack will present our plans for the refuge and explain why the commercial features in the other plan would be harmful. We will finish with a video that is really spectacular, if I do say so myself."

"Sounds wonderful. We'll be there early."

"You look beautiful, Raisha." Jack gave her a gentle peck on her neck and smiled into the mirror over her shoulder. "Let's get going." She grabbed her purse and hurried behind him into the station's car parked in the motel lot. When they arrived at the meeting place, a large auditorium in the basement of a church, the place was about a quarter filled and buzzing with conversations.

The conservation officer spotted them as they walked in. He hurried over. "Hello! We are so excited. Your seats are here in the front."

While Jack and the officer made arrangements with the projectionist, Raisha sat cross-legged, going over her speech in her mind. She wanted to avoid having to consult her notes. Then Dr. Edgar appeared and presented his two colleagues. They were gray-haired and distinguished looking, with kind faces.

The meeting began with formalities and announcements. When Raisha was introduced and took her place at the podium, someone stood in the back and yelled: "Who are you, miss, to tell us islanders what to do with our land? Raisha looked puzzled at the chairperson, who ran down the aisle to confront the man.

"Please give us a hearing before you condemn us," she said. "We are very sensitive to the needs of the islanders."

"Just how long have you been here?" the man continued, shouting.

"Less than a year, but I am not the issue. We have the support of the people in Waioo Island," she retorted confidently. This announcement caused a stir in the audience, and made it clear how crucial Iakano's involvement was.

The heckler left, and the presentation went on as scheduled. Dr. Edgar and his colleagues, added a valuable scholarly note by showing maps that illustrated how small the percentage of primeval forest was left on all of the islands, and Jack contrasted theirs and the government's invasive proposal for a nature reserve. The final applause was truly enthusiastic. A few questions followed: One person asked for how long the Anara bird was thought to be extinct. "The last sign of them was about fifty hears ago," answered Dr. Edgar. Another person asked for estimates of Anara's currently known population size. "This is not exactly known at the present. Although we have seen at least two breeding pairs," said Raisha.

After the meeting Jack and Raisha and the professors were surrounded by a group of young activists, "What is your next move? Are you in touch with any key politicians?" The questions were all similar, but the most important on was: "How can we help?"

While Jack took down names, phone numbers and e-mails of volunteers, Raisha turned to the conservation official: "Who was that man interrupting the meeting, and how did he know what I was going to say even before I opened my mouth?"

The official shrugged. "I never saw him before. I don't think he is a member of the Serra Club."

After most of the people left, Dr. Edgar took Raisha aside and whispered: "That heckler was one of Dr. Werner's students!"

"Why would a native person support ideas about commercializing that pristine region?", puzzled Raisha.

"My dear," replied the old professor, "Most people are more worried about making a living than preserving trees and birds."

25
An Offer

Raisha was grateful when the two professors asked to treat her for dinner. (Her meal ticket at the dorm had only one coupon left.) After they ordered, Dr. Edgar said: "That's quite a scoop for you to have discovered the Anara bird alive after all these years."

She dismissed the compliment and rubbed her tired eyes. "I am so disappointed with the response we've been getting... I expected the government to drag its feet, but you wouldn't believe how blithely they just pass off any action to seemingly endless committees."

Both professors nodded knowingly: "Sure we believe it. We've been around for a long time. We'd like to help. And we will write letters to editors. Is there anything else we can do?"

"Thank you. That will be a great help," she said sincerely. I'll let you know about anything else... After we regroup and strategize."

"Atta girl Keep on fighting!" Dr. Edgar patted her hand. (One of the other old professor's eyes drifted shut and his head started to nod.)

That evening in her dorm there was a message in her mailbox:

"Please come to my office first thing in the morning.'" It was signed with the illegible signature of Dr. Verner. It struck her odd that he should be delivering a written message, and signing it himself, instead of having his secretary contact her. She mulled over it all night: *What could he want. I am essentially done with him, and he isn't paying me anymore.... Wait, he probably wants me out of this dorm. Well, that's fine with me. I'll just stay with Jack.*

In the morning she ate a hearty breakfast, taking advantage of her remaining meal ticket. At nine she went to Verner's office. His door was open. He looked up from some papers on his desk and motioned her to sit down. After a minute he turned off his

83

computer, turned to her, whipped off his glasses, and addressed her with a concerned expression. "I am disturbed by the activity you and your friends are engaged in." He slipped on another pair of glasses, apparently ones for long distance. (Comprehension began seeping into her brain.) "I think you feel that you are on some sort of noble mission," he continued. (A slight smile flickered across his face, and quickly tightened into a frown.) "Whereas what you may do, is interfere with our project that would be a god-sent for the poor people of this island."

Raisha sat motionless, groping for words to express her feelings of distrust and disgust. *He has just usurped our discovery and made it into his project!* At the same time she still felt some subordination to the man who had given her, her first paying job. Finally with clenched fists she answered: "Dr. Verner, I too am disturbed, by the activity you and your friends are engaged in!", she mimicked.

Verner looked astonished, and for a second she thought that he would summarily dismiss her from his office. But then he looked out the window, and continued: "After much effort, we have obtained a large grant to proceed with our project and we are not going to let a neophyte with some activist friends stand in our way". He paused, red faced, apparently trying to gather his temper. After some time he started again: "We are prepared to make you an offer you might find very interesting: We wish to give you the position off Scientific Adviser to oversee any impact our Waikano Mountain project may have on the wildlife there. At a pretty hefty salary I might add."

"And what would my power be?" Raisha asked with a smirk.

"Why to make recommendations!"

"And who would follow them?"

"We are all anxious to do this right. Don't you know of my interests in ecology?"

"Fine," said Raisha. "I will accept your offer, provided I am given the power to nix anything that I would consider having a deleterious effect on the nature of the area. And I want that stated in writing!"

She could tell Verner was fuming. Eventually she got up and started for the door. "I am moving out of the dorm and will leave my new address with your secretary," she said over her shoulder.

"Be sure to drop off the keys to the station's wan!", he yelled after her. She scribbled the name of the motel where Jack was now staying (and where she too intended to stay now) on slip of paper and tossed it with the keys on the secretary's desk.

Outside she walked briskly, not really aiming anywhere in particular. She wound up on a beach. The pounding surf helped to calm her. Her cell's buzzing snapped her back to the present moment. It was Jack, sounding worried: "Where have you been? They told me you left your dorm some time ago."

"I'm on my way to you, Jack. It might take me about twenty minutes because I am walking." She tried to organize her mind by lining up their assets: *First there is Iakano and the support of his island; then the old professors and their pledge of help; finally some college kids from the Serra club. But what is that against many commercial interests, backed by the national government?*

Jack was waiting for her in front of the motel. As she greeted him, she was surprised to feel herself on the verge of tears. "Come on let's go to the diner," he said when he saw her.

"I can't eat anything."

"What happened? You look beat."

"An interesting choice of words. I hope they aren't prophetic."

"Stop it. Just tell me what's going on."

"Dr. Verner, (she couldn't bring herself to omit his title) has just offered me a job as Scientific Advisor for HIS Waikano Mountain project."

"Really? Why is that so bad? Maybe you could steer it to our interests from within."

"Be real, Jack. They would never let me nix anything substantial. In fact I told him that I want power to stop anything I

85

consider bad, and he reacted.... just as I thought he would...with a controlled tantrum."

"Still it might be useful to be in on the planning."

"You're still being naive, They would not let me in on that."

"OK, let's forget that."

"What can we do now?"

Jack sighed. "I've tried calling the Environmental Department again. The guy there is as frustrated as we are." He put his arm around her. Raisha felt it to be and imposition. Neither could think of anything else to say.

Just then, almost like the proverbial cavalry, the environmental official came running into view. "I have some great news for you!", he shouted from a distance, and when he reached them he continued: "There was a guy at the Serra meeting.... (He paused to catch his breath.)... from the National Ecology Society! As you probably know they have a popular TV program now." He sat down on the bench between them.

"So?" The impatient couple asked.

"It was just by chance they were in town to film some sort of festival."

"Will you get to the point."

"He said they want to come and film your bird and area, and if all goes well... they might make a big TV special out of it."

"Just exactly what would that involve", asked Raisha, trying to picture the production. " I..I mean we, especially Iakano and his people, don't want any large film crew truck or something coming into that pristine area."

Jack and the environmental guy seemed to not hear her. "What a great breakthrough!" beamed Jack. "When can we meet this fellow?"

"I said I would try to arrange a lunch. In fact I said that you would be at the Lapai Restaurant at noon today. I took the chance, you see, that I would be able to catch up with you."

"Great, we'll be there and we'll bring some of the stills we took!" Then looking at his watch, he turned to Raisha; "We better get moving."

The environment guy said apologetically, "I'm sorry but I can't join you now. (There is a board meeting which I am obliged to attend.) But please keep me informed."

After he left, Jack pulled Raisha's hand: "Come on we have to pick out the photos, There isn't much time!"

She refused to be budged. "How can you just assume that this is absolutely fine with me?"

"How can you hesitate?" He said sounding incredulous. "Don't you realize that this is the very thing we need? In fact, I didn't know how we could have proceeded without it."

"All I'm saying is that there are legitimate concerns, which Iakano and his people have. These are my concerns too, and I had hoped they were yours as well. Just promise me that you won't commit to anything that might damage that precious area!"

Why of course," Jack said frowning. Now would you please hurry up. She picked herself up wearily and followed jack into the motel.

26
Production

Raisha and Jack sat in a booth in the appointed restaurant. They were nervous and not in any mood for conversation. Menus lay before them, but both kept looking toward the entrance. A young man appeared maneuvering a large black shoulder bag through the door. Their eyes locked on him. He scanned the room made a beeline toward them.

"Dr. Endicott, I presume," he said, extending his free hand to Jack.

"I'm Raisha Endicott," she said coolly.

The young man fidgeted and looked at her with a pained expression, "I'm sorry they didn't tell me your first name." She waved it aside. He continued "I'm Steve Branoff of the Ecology Society." He put down his heavy shoulder bag, and lifted the press pass around his neck toward them both.

A waitress walked by with a load of dishes on her arm and glanced annoyed at the bag blocking the isle. "May I put this next you?" Steve asked Raisha, gesturing toward the bag. "It's my camera and I just couldn't leave it in the Jeep."

"Please," Raisha moved over. He placed the bag next to her and wiped his brow. "It's pretty hot on this island," he said as he settled himself next to Jack.

"You should loose that tie and get a pair of cotton pants," Jack said as the young man cleared his throat and loosened his tie. "Tell us what your role is and what are the plans of your organization," Jack continued somewhat impatiently.

"Well," Steve said with wide-eyed enthusiasm. "I'm all yours. Just show me what to film!" He sensed their skeptical mood.

"Look," he said scrutinizing each of their faces. "It's been hard for me to get where I am and I am not afraid of having to convince two more people that I can do my job."

The waitress appeared. "Are you finally going to order?"

Steve waived his hand. "Let's just get out of here. My jeep is gassed up and the day is young. Can we go to the site now?"

Raisha was the first to gather her wits. "We can't drive there! What equipment do you need?"

"You're looking at it." He gestured lovingly at the bag on the bench beside her. "She's heavy but I can carry it."

"OK, but first we must get you some suitable shoes and clothes."

No one said anything further, but as they walked out the door Raisha and Jack glanced at each other with shrugs that said: Who knows, this just might work.

They took the young photojournalist, to the motel room and Jack lent him some of his clothes. Luckily the two were almost the same size. They couldn't do the same about shoes, so they went to a store to buy him hiking boots and to pick up an extra sleeping bag, another canteen and some trail food. Eventually the three laid down on the two beds in Jack's room, planning to start their hike very early in the morning.

27
Confrontation

Steve was the first up the next day, but soon Raisha and Jack joined him. After breakfast in an adjacent diner, they set out. The going was tough for the new guy and they moved more slowly than usual, not only because Steve was not used to the humid heat and rough terrain, but also because he stopped often to film interesting scenery.

"You better quit that or you'll use up all your film."

"Not to worry I have many rolls."

They arrived at the cave late in the afternoon, Iakano looked wary, seeing the two males, but continued cooking.

"This is Steve," said Raisha. "He will be filming here. He works for the National Ecology Society. Hopefully the footage he gets will become part of a television special. We all think that would be very helpful to our cause." Aikano was dubious.

"I'll have to gather more things for our meal," Iakano said and walked off into the forest. Later he laid out pieces of cooked fish on four leaves and garnished then with fruits and vegetables. *He could be a real chef,* thought Raisha as she munched the delicious food.

Shortly thereafter the exhausted, newly-arrived trio fell soundly asleep. Iakano replenished the platform for the bird-god and carefully made sure all embers of a fire were cold. Then he too went to sleep on a bed made of woven grass cushioned underneath by leaves.

Raisha and Jack woke at about seven and were surprised to find both Iakano and Steve gone. They spotted the two early birds about a third way down the canyon. Steve, his hair tousled, was filming the view below. They decided to join them.

"The view is even better at sunset, Steve," said Raisha as she and Jack approached. Then for a while all four just drank in the fresh morning air.

Iakano pointed up the hill toward the cave and platform: "They should be coming for their breakfast about now." Steve, eager for what should come next, moved up the slope first. The rest followed. Suddenly a shot rang out. Instinctively they all hit the ground.

"It's near the cave." Jack whispered," Some of them wanted to run up there, but Iakano held them back. He crouched down flat and carefully crawled toward the noise. The others imitated his slow moves.

They heard: "Hey will you look at that!" And moving even closer they saw two burly guys in camouflage overalls, pointing rifles up toward the tree above the feeding platform. Anara took off. Several shots rang throughout the valley.

"I think I wounded it," one of the shooters said, and both hunters struggled through the brush, firing off more rounds as they went.

Suddenly an Anara couple alighted next to Iakano. The birds seemed enormous, waddling on the ground. One of them was wounded. They huddled near Iakano as if sensing he could protect them. Steve couldn't suppress audible intakes of breath, while with trembling hands he held on to his camera. It made a whirling sound that somehow no-one had heard earlier under normal circumstances.

Iakano, next to a bush with abundant green berries, turned to Raisha: "Do you have your pocket knife?" She nodded and pulled her Swiss Army knife from her pocket. He fashioned two straight sticks into dart-like spears, and rubbed juice from the green berries on their sharpened tips. Then he slithered noiselessly toward the two intruders.

The hunters were so engrossed in searching for their prey, that they didn't notice Iakano until he stood. At that moment he deftly threw the stick-darts at their necks. They were about to point their guns at him when each collapsed.

Iakano motioned for the others to join him. "Go find more of this vine," he said as he pulled a strand of it from a tree. "We must secure them before they wake up."

They tied up the two hunter's hands behind their back, and carried them up to the cave, where they propped them against the wall of the cave, just as they were coming to.

"What the hell?!" one hunter groaned.

Jack, assuming a lawyer's tone said: "We are arresting you for endangering our lives."

"What are you? Some crazy, hippie nuts?" Said the other hunter, after he tried and failed to free his hands. He looked at Iakano, who was now calmly stoking a fire. "You are going to jail for this!"

After struggling for some time, both hunters became resigned that they couldn't undo their bonds. Then Iakano and Jack blindfolded the bewildered pair using strips of cloth. "We are going to remove you from these premises," Jack explained, "and we want to be sure you would not be able to easily find your way back here."

Raisha and Jack took up the hunter's guns and made the burly pair march ahead of them, toward town. Steve followed them, still filming, but Iakano stayed at the cave. As they neared the edge of the forest, a policeman, who was patrolling the area, halted the strange group. "Drop those guns!" He ordered, fingering his own gun in its holster. Jack and Raisha handed the hunter's guns over. Steve, who was some distance behind them, hid behind a large tree. "Just what is going on here?" the policeman growled.

"Help us officer," the hunters squealed.

Jack answered trying to sound official: "We made a citizens' arrest because these men were behaving dangerously."

The policeman was incredulous. "Tell it to a judge," he said, and handcuffed Raisha and Jack.'

At the headquarters the police were equally skeptical of Jack's account. The indignant hunters filed charges of assault.

Jack arranged bail, using his credit card, and tried to calm Raisha: "We have a solid case, don't worry," Later they were happy to see Steve, who slipped into the motel cautiously after dark.

28
Courtroom

"We demand retribution!", yelled one of the hunters. He was interrupting the prosecuting attorney, whom he had hired. Seeing the annoyed faces of the judge and foreman, he continued in a milder tone. "Mr Atkinson and I have suffered a great deal because of these crazy activists!"

"Sit down. Any more outbursts and you will be charged with contempt of court" said the judge and turned to the attorney: "Please continue."

"As I was saying, Mr. Sweeney and Mr. Atkinson were on Waikano Mountain. They had valid licenses permitting the taking of small game. The defendants and their friends, one of them a primitive native!" (He paused for emphasis.) "poisoned them, tied them up, and blindfolded them. Thus bound they escorted my clients at gunpoint, out of the woods. Where, just by chance, a local police officer saw them and arrested the defendants. (He looked at Raisha and Jack with contempt.) "We charge Drs. Raisha Endicott and John Soltano with assault and reckless endangerment of Mr. Sweeney and Mr. Atkinson and, we ask for a maximum punishment."

The courtroom hummed with conversation. The judge struck his gavel "We'll hear the defense attorney's statement now."

Steve rose and adjusted his notes. "Your honor. I will present evidence that the accusers were attempting to kill an extremely rare bird, one that has importance not only to scientists, but is also a sacred symbol to the indigenous people of these islands."

"That may be", the judge replied, "but it doesn't excuse the violent and humiliating treatment they received."

"Your Honor, we had no choice. These hunters also threatened us with bodily harm."

"Objection!" announced the prosecutor, this is a lie that they are making up to excuse their abominable conduct."

"I'm afraid you're saying so, Mr. Soltano, is not enough to convince me that real threats were not made by you and your friends."

"I am prepared to show you a video of what happened." The courtroom buzzed. " I wish to call Steve Branoff to the witness stand."

"State your name and occupation," said the clerk, as Steve came up, carrying a laptop computer.

"Steve Branoff, photographer for *Ecology Magazine*."

"Please explain your connection with this case"

"I was with Drs. Endicott and Soltano on Waikano Mountain for the purpose of documenting the bird in question. Thus my camera was running at the time of the incident. I have the footage here in my computer and I can show it to the court."

The observers in the courtroom became excited and even the judge looked impressed by this turn of events. After a short pause he said: "Very well, we will resume tomorrow to give you time to set up a screen for projecting this documentation."

A reporter bolted out of the room.

Early the next day a large crowd gathered outside of the courthouse. They couldn't all get inside, but that did not deter their enthusiasm. A front-page story in a local, liberal paper reported all the testimony that had been given, under the title: "Protecting A Sacred Bird." Another, right-leaning paper, carried the same story on page three, headlined "Controversy about Access Rights." Both stories stated that the defendants were about to present video evidence. Even the TV news carried a note about it, which featured a painted picture of Anara, that a young reporter found in an old textbook. (He had learned its name after he telephoned Raisha.)

Jack and Raisha didn't get much sleep, because they were constantly on the phone. Apparently Steve had contacted his editors and they in turn called other outlets interested in wildlife protection. Everyone smelled a good story!

Walking up the courtroom steps the next day, Raisha and Jack were temporarily blinded by flashes from reporters' cameras. Inside, the press box was filled to overflowing.

Steve had already turned on his power point computer presentation, showing a long view of the beach at Waikano Mountain. The foto showed up clearly even without the lights being dimmed, and elicited admiring stares from the lucky few who got into the courtroom.

After the judge called the session to order, the prosecuting attorney rose and said: "Your honor, I object to this unnecessary propaganda. We are not here to offer travel entertainment, but to determine whether the defendants had any reason to attack these legitimate hunters."

The judge seemed to smirk a bit and ordered the picture turned off. He turned to Steve, "Are you ready with the video?"

Steve nodded and began: "I was with the defendants, half way down the slope toward the beach you had just seen, when we heard gunshots. I will let the video I took thereafter, tell the rest of the story."

The video began dramatically with gunshots, and frightened voices of Raisha and Jack: "It's coming from the cave!" Raisha, Iakano and Jack were then seen crawling slowly up the canyon.

The audience in the courtroom gasped when Iakano in the foreground, was suddenly joined by two large, orange birds. The camera focused on a bleeding wound of one of the birds. Then the focus swung toward the cave area, showing the two hunter defendants, dressed in camouflage, moving toward them with guns raised. The hunters fired several gunshots, which could be heard whizzing by the camera, the focus of which swung toward the sky.

Steve paused the projector. "Those gunshots passed right over us. They missed us only because we were all flat on the ground. Soon after this Iakano threw his little, hand-made spears, drenched with a juice of a local berry known by the natives to have anesthetic powers."

The court room observers were riveted when Steve powered up the projector again The next scene showed the two hunters unconscious, with their hands tied, behind their backs. They started to come to and one yelled, "What the hell?" Jack was heard saying "We're arresting you for endangering our lives." This was followed by: "What are you, some crazy hippie nuts?", from one of the hunters, and "You're going to jail for this," from the other.

When the projector was turned off, the prosecutor spoke again: "Your honor, this video presents no real proof that either of my clients fired at the defendants. How do we know that this video has not been doctored up? However, it clearly shows the physical abuse these activists inflicted on my clients."

The judge rubbed his chin. "We will have this evidence reviewed by an expert before we make a decision. "Please turn your video over to the court, Mr Branoff."

Steve complied and the court was dismissed until further notice.

When they stepped outside, Raisha and Jack had several microphones thrust at them. "What were you all doing up on Waikato Mountain?" asked one reporter.

"We are trying to protect a rare bird, sacred to the endogenous population here." Raisha answered. As a naturalist and because I have consulted with several experts, I can assure you that the only way to accomplish this is to declare the Waikano Mountain area a nature preserve." She tried to continue with details of what the reserve would entail, but most of the reporters were not ready to hear long explanations. They were trying to meet deadlines.

"Was that bird badly hurt?', a female reporter called out.

Jack answered, "We think that it will recover, because our friend Iakano treated it with native plant remedies immediately."

"What are your plans now?', asked another reporter.

"We will continue to press our case", Steve answered.

"Incidentally those hunters were in violation of local ordinances by wearing camouflage outfits. The law clearly states that each hunter must wear bright orange to help avoid accidents. There may be other violations these people committed."

After the crowd of reporters and onlookers dispersed, a well-dressed older man approached Raisha and Jack.

"I represent a party, who wishes to help you," he said as he handed each of them a card. (On one side it just said *Philantropy,* and on the reverse it listed an 800 number.) "Can we go somewhere to talk?"

Raisha, Jack and Steve were curious. They and the well-dressed man went to a cafe across the street. As they settled into a booth the man said:" My employer is prepared to help you in any way possible," he said and added: "Money is no object."

Raisha opened her mouth, but no words came out. Steve grinned and asked, "What do we have to do?"

"Please come to meet my employer at his home tonight," and slipped Steve another card with an address. "Shall we say eight PM?" Then he got up, bowed and left.

29
A Valuable Player

Raisha staggered a bit as she got out of the motel's shower. (It had been a harrowing plight of arrest and a tension filled day in the courtroom.) And now they were gearing up for another encounter, one with that mysterious and promising stranger. She couldn't face the hamburger Jack brought, but just gorged on a calorie laden milkshake.

Arriving at the address given them by the "philanthropy" representative, they gasped at a mansion, barely visible beyond the ornate entrance and long driveway. After they answered a query from a pleasant voice, the gate slowly opened. Perfume of flowering trees wafted through the air during the drive to the house. Two butler types stood at the head of a curve before the mansion's door. One showed them in and the other offered to park their car.

The inside was opulent, as expected, but what surprised them was the amount of native artifacts everywhere. "The master will see you shortly. May I get you some refreshment?" the indoor butler asked.

"Perhaps some coffee," both Jack and Raisha answered.

An older man slipped quietly into the room. He was dressed in a muted, brocade dinner jacket. "I realize you must be tired after your court appearance," he said as he motioned them to sit on a comfortable sofa, next to a resplendent fireplace. "So I will try to make it brief: I have decided to put any amount of money required at your disposal for the purpose of accomplishing your goal of saving whatever part of Waikano Mountain you consider necessary to preserve Anara. " They held their breath all during the time the man pronounced that long sentence.

The man continued, breaking a long pause: "Oh forgive me I haven't properly introduced myself. I am Dr. Maier." He handed them a calling card with his private phone number, and added humbly, "My title is really nothing. I wrote a thesis on native pottery ten years ago."

Raisha, skeptical but hopeful said: "Our main problem is that the government is now backing a proposal for that area that is sure to disrupt....no - I meant.. to decimate the fragile ecology of the region."

"Not to worry, Dr Maier said, nodding. "I have already sent my people to Washington. "I know many key elements there and am confident we can have those plans changed. Your work with the *Ecology Magazine* is sure to be very helpful." Smiling he added: "You know the mood of the nation is leaning to backing green projects now." He rang a silver bell and the butler reappeared. "Please bring us a coffee tray.".

"I worry about some of the population here objecting to loss of revenue," Jack interjected.

"That is a small worry. But you know I have worked with the people here before. And they are usually more than happy to work with me. It is the outside developers, looking to make a quick buck, that lead to wrong decisions that are harmful in the long run."

"We have support from the indigenous people living on Waioo Island," added Raisha.

"I am aware of that. Quite remarkable considering how reclusive they usually are."

He seems to know everything, thought Raisha as their host poured coffee and offered them some exquisite little cakes. They took them gratefully. After they finished, Maier stood. "Now I am sure you will be glad to go and rest. We will discuss details another day." He smiled and helped Raisha to get up. Then he ordered the butler to get their car.

During the ride home Raisha asked, "Do you think this is on the level?"

"We'll find out. But if he's who I think he is, our prayers have been answered," said Jack.

In the motel, Jack called a friend in Washington. "Would you do me a favor?... Please look up a Dr. Maier (that's M A I E R), who may have some expertise on South Sea Island Culture and some influence in Washington."

The friend called back after about thirty minutes. Jack's face brightened after he answered the phone. "Really, that is amazing and explains a lot." He hung up, and Raisha looked at him expectedly. "Our benefactor is a descendant of the man who founded the Waioo Island refuge. The family is one of the richest in the world. Their money was made originally by exporting tropical wood and now they export a variety of farm products - the usual fruits and plants."

"I don't know much about it," sighed Raisha, "but I do know that the wood industry wiped out many indigenous species, and now the farmers here are often in conflict with environmentalists.

"At least Maier is on our side. Good thing he inherited his ancestors' guilty conscience."

30
Resolution

The next day newspapers were full of the trial. "Here's an interesting write up," Jack shouted, as Raisha emerged from the motel's bathroom, drying her hair with a towel. "It's an editorial supporting your position of establishing a nature reserve." He quoted: "The time has come for politicians to start taking environmental scientists and activists seriously. We have already seen some of their dire predictions come true. We implore people and corporations to look beyond their next year's profit margins!'"

"That's good!", agreed Raisha.

"Wait, here's the best part: "The latest skirmish at City Court concerning a sacred bird at Waikano Mountain is giving us a local opportunity to do what's right."

"O, oh !" Raisha worried. "That may not be good. It might attract all kinds of riff-raff to the site."

"That mountain is a big place." Jack tried to reassure her. "I'm betting the most people will get tired in the first few miles of the necessary hike. They thankfully do not describe the exact location further."

Forced by the judge to stay in town, they spent their time walking along the beach trying to stay calm. Happily they were called back to the courtroom the very next day.

The judge's smile seemed encouraging. He called a video expert to the stand and questioned the witness himself: "What is your name and business?"

"I am Alexander Nimikoff. I own a video firm. We produce videos and service video equipment."

"We appreciate your service in this case," the judge continued.

"Would you please tell the court what you found by analyzing Mr. Branoff's video?"

"Well it would be extremely easy to tell if there were any 'modification' of the original take, and we found none."

"Did you make any findings about the gunshots heard on the tape?"

"Yes, they were aimed directly at the person taking the video."

The courtroom hummed and several reporters started dialing their bureaus.

"Thank you," the judge said after he banged his gavel to quell the noise. "In view of this testimony, I rule that the defendants were justified in the precautions they took to protect themselves. The court is dismissed." And he banged his gavel a final time.

The hunters were livid. Their lawyer just closed his folder.

Reporter's outside asked rather inane questions, like: "How do you feel about your victory?" They didn't seem concerned about the conservation issue, so after a brief exchange, Jack held up his hand and pleaded, "Dr. Endicott really needs to rest after this ordeal." So the crowd dispersed.

"Let's celebrate!" Jack said taking Raisha's hand.

"No Jack, I have to go see Iakano at the cave as soon as I can."

"For heaven sake, why? The guys in his element. There's nothing we need him for now."

"Oh jack, how can you talk as if he were just an object. He is after all, the key person involved here and must be worried about everything."

Jack eyed her suspiciously and considered trying further persuasion, but relented. "Don't stay there too long....there are plans we have to make."

103

31
In Their Element

It was barely dawn when Raisha, feeling anxious, packed her backpack, and left a note with her cell number for Jack and Steve, who were still asleep. (She had fully charged her cell phone during the night, and hoped it would have reception on Waikano.) Then she slipped out of the room and walked toward the mountain.

The morning freshness calmed her somewhat. Se recalled Jack's phrase, "in his element. *I feel better in that element myself,* she thought, as she took a deep breath and stepped into the forest.

Finally reaching the cave, she felt a letdown, for Iakano was nowhere in sight. Near the feeding platform, she spotted a flat rock with many wood chips all around it. On the rock lay her Swiss army knife and a wood carving in progress. She bent down to inspect it.

To her delight she realized that it resembled her face. A faint noise made her turn. She saw Iakano coming her way.

She stood. "I have wonderful news."

He smiled broadly, and led her to their favorite spot at the edge of the cliff.

"We now have a very wealthy backer, who said he would finance all the expenses for the nature reserve," she said beaming. (He did not respond with happy smiles as she had hoped.) "Most importantly he asserts that he has clout with the big government, enough to defeat another odious plan that Verner has been pushing."

"What happened with the hunters?" He asked, ignoring the news.

"Well, Jack and I were arrested at the edge of the forest." (Iakano turned and clutched her shoulder.) "No, don't worry. Even that worked out. You see the trial produced much publicity and... well that's how we found our benefactor." He leaned closer to her and after gently lifting her chin, kissed her on the mouth. The kiss surprised her and made her heart race. She wound her arms around him and kissed him back.

"Tell me about your friend, Jack," he said.

"There's nothing to discuss. He is truly just a friend. I...." He interrupted her with another kiss and she returned it, this time with passion. Then she happily nestled in his arms, feeling that she could stay there forever. He moved some hair from across her face and stroked her head.

"Let's go down for a swim," he said pulling her to her feet. They practically flew down to the beach, with Iakano carrying her over some rough patches. On the beach they both threw off all their clothes. In the warm water, to her delight, bright yellow and blue fishes swam around their legs. Iakano picked some seaweed and the fishes took it from his hands, like domesticated pets.

As if in a dream they moved to the fresh water spring and splashed each other like two children. After Raisha put on her clothes and Iakano fastened on a loincloth, they sat leaning against a boulder. Finally Raisha said: "You know Iakano you never really explained to me why you came to leave your island to live with the newcomers long enough to learn our language."

Iakano sighed." I was eighteen...it was ten years ago. I had been sheltered on our island.... Even then my people were sending out young men to search for Anara."

He got up and started pacing. "I volunteered for one of those forays and was allowed to go on it because I was particularly good at paddling a canoe. Our search group split up and by chance I ran into a young lady." (He paused and frowned.)

"Don't stop now." Raisha interjected. "This is just starting to get interesting. "Was this lady beautiful?"

"Well she had beautiful hair.... but not as beautiful as yours. Anyway, she was part of a hippie commune...and ...well she took me to where they lived... I can't believe that I just stayed with them.... They used a lot of drugs." He looked away and seemed ashamed to continue.

"Don't worry, "I won't reproach you for anything you did when you were young and foolish."

"I soon became tired and desperate," he continued. "We had to perform dances for the tourists and even..... I mean romance some of the ladies. I want you to know I never did that part, but I knew some of the others would do anything to earn money." He picked up the pace of his narrative, obviously hoping to get it over with.

"Finally I managed to get a small paying job with a fellow who rented out canoes. He let me sleep in a shed and gave me food. I asked him if I could buy one of his canoes. He laughed at first but eventually decided to give me a canoe that needed extensive repair. I worked on it for moths." (His eyes started to glisten.) "It was a terrible time for me. I longed to return to my people. I was sick of the fumes and the dirt, the tourists and their music, their noisy cars and radios... Finally my canoe was ready and I set out one night."

"How did you know your way back?"

"We are all taught to follow the stars. That's why I had to set out at night. When I got back, some of the people were happy to see me. But the elders were skeptical. Still I was allowed to stay. Even now, many of them have suspicions.."

The next weeks became a kind of domestic bliss for Iakano and Raisha. They worked together in making delicious meals. He taught her about edible plants and she became proficient in cooking fish. They took excursions into the surrounding woods, teaching each other from their different perspectives, about the various life they encountered. Each morning he would bring her breakfast on a large green leaf. She came to expect being awakened by this loving tribute.

One day she woke disappointed because he was not around. Then to her relief, he showed up with the usual breakfast. "I was delayed because I wanted to find this," he said and handed her a lovely white orchid.

She smiled and brought the exquisite blossom to her face. It had a rich, sweet fragrance. "Our women wear these behind their left ear when they are married," he said shyly.

Her love for him swelled as understanding seeped into her mind, and she resolutely placed the wedding symbol behind her ear. "The left one, right?" she asked. He beamed and made sure it was secure. (The delicate orchid had a long curved nectary that fit perfectly behind her ear.)

"What a wonderful morning!" he said standing up.

They ran down to the beach along the now, well-worn path. Reaching the beach they threw off all their clothes as usual, and ran into the warm surf. They both sank to their knees. His fondling of her neck and breasts merged with the gently lapping waves. She never felt more alive. "I love you," he whispered... She clung to him tightly as her world merged with him into one gorgeous wave. They slowly recovered. She thought: *We will have beautiful children.*

As they washed in the fresh water stream, a call rang out from the top of the cliff: "Raisha, where are you?" It was Jack.

She couldn't stop herself from giving Iakano more kisses. He hugged and kissed her back, but finally said smiling. "We better get dressed and go meet your friend." Before the climb she made sure the white orchid was still secure behind her ear.

At the top she was surprised to see their philanthropist benefactor.

"Dr. Maier insisted on coming along to see the famous site," Jack explained. Maier eyed her intently and smiled acknowledging the orchid symbol.

"I am happy to see you again," Raisha said to Dr. Maier, and without hesitation then added: "This is Iakano, my husband."

"Your what?" Exclaimed jack. "Next you'll be telling us that the bird-god performed the ceremony!"

In contrast to Jack's outburst, the older man said calmly, "May I congratulate you!". Then he kissed Raisha's hand, and shook Iakano's. "My best wishes for a long and happy future."

Jack glared at Raisha, who was now blushing. Maier, sensing a pending dispute, steered Iakano toward the feeding platform. "Would you show me the details of your setup here?"

"You can't be serious," Jack exclaimed when they were alone. She looked away to the horizon. "Just don't come running back to me when this crazy affair of yours ends."

"Iakano and I are really in love," Raisha said, and added triumphantly, "I hope that we have already conceived a child!"

"Oh, wouldn't that make your parents happy!" Jack smirked.

The philanthropist and Iakano came back before Raisha could respond.

Maier said amiably. "We all should return to town now. There is still much to arrange."

"It's difficult for me to leave this place, Iakano worried. "I must do all I can to protect Anara! There have already been intruders here."

"I have taken some precautions," said Maier. My people are now patrolling the outskirts. And they are setting up lasers that can be tripped by any large animals crossing them. Since there are no large animals here except humans, we are sure the area will be secure."

Then seeing their incredulous faces he explained further. "We also have a way of hooking up with an orbiting satellite. And the laser devices run on batteries with very long lives. Eventually we will have set up a solar generator to replenish their power easily."

Raisha thought: *Accumulating so much money can accomplish things that seem impossible otherwise. I wonder if this can be done without hurting others."*

Iakano nevertheless chose to stay at the cave. "I can be more useful here," he explained as he hugged Raisha goodbye."

"I'll be back soon," she whispered. She knew she would miss him terribly, but was proud of his dedication.

32
Celebration

It took weeks before all the official papers to make their nature reserve a reality, were signed and filed. The waiting seemed interminable to Raisha. During this time Jack spent most of his time with Dr. Maier, making plans and clearing legal matters. Both Jack and Maier were respectful of Raisha and always waited for her to review any plans before finalizing them. She in turn did the same with Iakano.

Raisha became busy with production of a TV special for the *Nature Society*. They had enough footage and stills made by her and Steve, so returning to the site was not necessary, but they insisted on adding an interview of her, in which she tried to satisfy both conservation and commercial aspects.

As before, there were two sides offering suggestions and objections for the refuge. Each side had its extremes: purists who didn't want any non-natives messing with their heritage, and extreme materialists who thought natural areas just stood in the way of prosperity and jobs. These two sides could only be resolved by compromise, which was helped by the sensitive portrayal of the reserve made in the TV special. The result was that there were to be tours coming to the larger area of the nature reserve, on the periphery. Also on the periphery there would be a lodge. However, no vehicles would be allowed in the rest of the reserve, and the nesting area, near the cliff, would be completely off limits to anyone without a special permit.

At last, a celebration banquet was set and Raisha went back to the cave to invite Iakano. She had to plead: "It just wouldn't be the same without you. Once it's over I'll come back here to stay with you always."

He relented, saying: "Promise me you won't make me wear something like a dinner jacket."

"Well, I'd love to see you dressed in one," she teased, "but of course you can wear anything... Well maybe not anything, I don't want others to gawk at your gorgeous muscles."

After making love and eating dinner, they both slept soundly under the stars. The next day in town Raisha took him to a clothier, and with money advanced her by Dr. Maier, bought him a light summer suit. They found a shirt for him and a matching long gown for her. Both had a lovely floral design, rendered in violets and greens. Then they checked into a luxurious hotel, where their room was paid for by their benefactor. (Jack had been offered the same lodging by Maier, but he preferred to remain in the old motel.)

On the night of the banquet Raisha looked resplendent in her new evening gown. Her hair was up in a graceful twist and a white orchid was lovely behind her left ear. She and Iakano were met by a barrage of camera flashes as they stepped out of a limousine, provided by Maier. "Do you have a statement we could use?" a reporter asked hopefully and several of them pushed microphones in front of her face. Jack stepped up to her side, and took her arm trying to steer her away from the reporters.

"Wait a minute," she wrestled her arm back and faced them. "We are celebrating a hard-won settlement. It came at a large price," she paused for emphasis, "not just in hard work but also because I still have some fear of possible consequences... Like...too many people coming to a place that must remain sacred." She wanted to continue but a glance from Jack made her pause. "Thank you," she continued, we couldn't have done this without the publicity you gave us." Then she picked up her gown with both hands and steering clear of Jack's help, hurried into the banquet room.

Inside she was greeted with applause and took her place between Jack and Iakano at the head of the room. The meal consisted of adapted native dishes served on plates that resembled leaves. The conversation during the meal was sparse. Jack kept busy working the guest tables. Iakano sensing Raisha's tenseness remained silent.

Jack came over, flushed with the success he apparently had in the negotiations he had just made. "Come on Raisha, let's go have a drink at the bar with some people."

"I just can't Jack. Please make my excuses," said Raisha standing close to Iakano. She had her hand on her abdomen. Jack pressed together his lips and walked away.

Printed in the USA
CPSIA information can be obtained
at www.ICGtesting.com
LVHW020501251023
761974LV00056B/1172